Molly's Curse

J.D. Warner

Molly's Curse

THE
UNSEEING
EYE

TALLINN, 2021

This is a work of fiction. Names, characters, businesses, places, events, locales, and incidents are either the products of the author's imagination or used in a fictitious manner. Any resemblance to actual persons, living or dead, or actual events is purely coincidental, except when said persons explitictly asked and/or literally begged to be included in the story. The author bears no responsibility for any fictitious characters' fate, good or ill; of this the consenting parties have been notified.

First paperback edition,
Published in 2021 by The Unseeing Eye
in Tallinn, Estonia
www.theunseeingeye.com

Cover concept by Attila Orosz
Cover photo "Clifftops" by Tamara Knight

The Unseeing Eye is a publishing imprint of
AtlanticOmnibus oü
10130 Kiriku 6, Tallinn, Estonia
www.atlanticomnibus.com

Atlantic Omnibus

ISBN 978-9916-9589-6-4

"Love in action is a harsh and
dreadful thing compared with
love in dreams."

Fyodor Dostoevski

Chapter 1

Cliff Capers

I WAS RUDELY WOKEN at the tender hour of 4:30AM by the sound of someone rummaging in my drawers.

Getting up onto one elbow, I gave the back of my son's head a disdainful look before asking, "Gavin, what are you doing? Do you know what the time is?"

"Sorry, Mum," he muttered without an apologetic syllable in sight, moving down a drawer and peering through my petticoats and panties.

I

"The frilly ones are at the back," I said, flopping back down, one arm over my face to keep out the light from the corridor. "Is there something you want to tell me regarding this underwear obsession; to tell your lovely wife?"

He grunted a laugh. "I just think when Vana emptied these drawers for you to move in, she must've missed something, 'cause I can't find it anywhere."

"It?"

"A notebook," he said, turning his attentions to the bottom drawer. "Tiddly thing, half A6 size, whatever that is. You haven't seen it around, have you?"

"Gavin, I've been here a while now. Any notebook, tiny or otherwise, would have come to light by now, don't you think?" I yawned widely. "Perhaps the kids took it to draw in. How important can it possibly be if you haven't needed it until now, and why's the info not in your lovely shiny computer?"

"Some things are safer not in a PC. It was a client list for the last place I worked. Kept it just in case, and now the boss needs something I think's in

there. Actually, I thought it was in the safe but…"
His stressed voice faded out and rummaging
ensued in the tall boy instead.

"Have you asked Vana yet?" I sighed. "Your
father always lost things and I always found them.
June says Henry's just the same. So pop off and
shut the door on the way out, there's a darling."
Rolling onto my front, I closed my eyes into the
pillow, though I doubted I'd get to sleep again.

"Vana?" His voice echoed down the corridor
that connects my flat to the house. Then the door
clicked shut as I longed to hear him say, "Love
you, Mum," like in the days of old, but the words
never came.

"Love you, Gavin," I whispered into the early
morning's waking drone, missing the loving child
he had once been, lamenting the man who had
grown up out of my sight. Time could not be
reclaimed.

On the really quiet nights back in Hartpury, the
silence could get so thick your heartbeat was your
only company, but outside my seaside window the
world was beginning to wake, seagulls up since

first light. Every morning here in Little Kerton-on-Sea, I had to deal with family activity, people's loud voices, Gavin and Vana rushing around to go to work... It was another noisy world entirely.

I was glad to be under Gavin's aegis, but I pined for the peaceful presence of Hartpury woods. But one rarely gets everything one wants in life, and this seaside town had to be better than where I had lived, because my family was here, my grandchildren, my new life safe from harm.

'Let me sleep a little more,' I prayed, 'for soon my three grandchildren will whirl into my bedroom like the winds of wrath, and leap onto me if I'm not up to get their breakfasts.'

⁓

Oh, I am so sorry; do forgive me. I was so shocked by my son's lack of manners I forgot my own. I haven't introduced myself. I am Molly, born Miss Turner, then Mrs Marshman, and now Ms Smith, aged seventy five. I wanted to live by the seaside and got my wish when my son took me into his family after an awful hoo-ha with drug dealers near Gloucester. Although I don't regret the move, trying to hide just like my son is in the witness protection programme is a boring life.

I've been here over a year now and, despite that overwhelming urge to get here and live here and have a new life here, what I have found is that what you want is not always what you need, and desire for new-ness and safety can quickly fade.

In my mind's eye I had seen the seaside as sunshine, blue water and softly lapping waves, very much like the picture that hangs over my sofa, but Kerton's not like that at all. What I now experience daily is the sticky-salty sea spray in my hair the moment I step out of the house, and permanently having to dress like it's deep mid-winter, not to mention the new rash of wrinkles I have garnered from walking with my face scrunched up against the prevailing wind-blown sand.

Yes, sand at the seaside—how dare it be there.

It gets everywhere. I care for my grandchildren and I could call all of them Sandy. Here is lovely sweet Myha, six-years-old with cafe-au-lait curls, and Minnie, her identical twin. Collin is much taller, older at eight, a rather awkward child who thinks he knows everything and hates being corrected, and talks back to me all the time. He runs me ragged but I do love his spark.

The children like nothing more at the end of a school day than to eschew the village playground with swings and fancy apparatus and instead run down to the beach and build frigid castles and raid rock pools that still have a thin sheet of ice on them at 3:30PM. And I am the one who cleans up after the children, who vacuums the sand out of carpets, and shakes beds and the boy's pockets and everything.

Vana is a fiery woman of whom I am too polite to ask the whys and wherefores of her family origins. Her English is natural but finely peppered with words of her own language, and if you get her mad she'll spout incomprehensibly. I think Collin gets his awkward attitude from her.

He's making me miserable, that grandson of mine. I wanted to love these children, to hug them and play with them, to make up for so many lost years, but instead I have to face his overt cheekiness along with my disillusionment with the seaside.

I've even gone so far as to get a hearing aid, sans battery. My hearing is fine, you see, but the family doesn't know that, so I can leave it on the side and hear Collin's plots and plans without him knowing I can hear. He also likes to run off with it to annoy me, though it's become more of a game lately. It's just my way of getting one-upmanship on the child. Am I a sneaky woman? I prefer to think that what I do is all for the good of the children.

Gavin says I have to accept that Collin is Vesuvius, boiling with hot words and ideas, and Little Kerton is Antarctica, four months of sunny activity and eight months of the cold, cold wind that comes off the sea, and I know he just wants me to stop complaining.

I suspect he is fed up with me already, even though I have taken on the task of housekeeper and childminder while he and Vana work. I feel I am Nana-the-irreplaceable, the mighty organiser without whom this family would fall apart, and I wonder every day how they managed before I came back into their lives. I arrived with a lot of money so I don't think the cost bothers him, but

I am trying to figure out what's wrong. There is something about his attitude, the odd small remark that hurts me. I had been dumb enough to imagine us running into each other's arms to the resounding chords of movie music. But although we had hugged then, conversation nowadays is sparse. Hello and goodbye and let's rummage in your drawers at an ungodly hour—and even when I ask what's wrong, he has to 'rush' and the issue is never resolved.

My mother used to tell me I was destined for greatness. I could never believe that. I felt at the time it was something that all decent parents said to encourage their offspring, but the best 'greatness' I ever felt was when I dropped a man down a well, and I'm pretty sure she didn't mean that, or that she would have approved of it—even though it had been to save my own life.

⁓

At the end of the school day, the children walked in front of me, filled with chattering post-school excitement, and traipsed down the wooden cliff stairs to the rocky beach. It is at least fun to beach-comb while they play, the twins throwing sand at each other—which I have told them not to do a thousand times and have now given up saying. They'll have to learn the hard way.

I like the way you can walk to everything here. The shop sells a good selection of items, including fossils, and is also a Post Office at select times. There's a lovely pub overlooking the sea, and a spectacular new village hall, and I really like that there are very few residents out of season. Fewer people means less rubbish, though I know that will change once we get some tourists as the weather warms up. Not many visitors, because the beach is hardly Costa Del Sol, and we have no town novelties to hold anyone, though the fossil hunters like the cliffs; no spooky caves or joke shops or souvenir huts or ice cream parlours. The old restaurant will likely have to shut this year if the spring storms cause more landslips in its area, and if the shop doesn't have what you want you have to drive or bus to the bigger towns inland.

While the girls set to their favourite occupation of building sand-castles, Collin wandered around on the cold beach, his thick brown hair ruffled by the wind, finding more stony things for his collection and filling his school bag with them; and with sand. Did I mention the sand that gets everywhere? It would be in his school books too, and I'd have to shake them out onto the porch when we got home. I cannot deny I found looking after the children hard work. I loved the interaction with them but, not being as young as I used to be, my energy levels had dipped—but Lord knows I will never admit to being old.

The winter waves were grey and foamy, and the sea roared like a petulant bear to the accompaniment of shrill gulls' cries. I shivered despite my coat and scarf and all the other warming woolly stuff.

Then I heard a voice from above me.

The cliffs over the beach are not majestic towering stacks, they're a sloping thirty degree angle of messed up rock falls and slippage and mud and clay and sand and everything else. On the cliff top above where I stood, dozens of feet away on the angle, the spire of our small abandoned church could just be seen. Coastal and cliff erosion has taken down most of the graveyard and the sea literally carried away its bones, the sweet little church replete with danger: do not enter signs. A dozen more years and its own stony-bones will rest in the sea.

I looked up at a second loud voice. Way above me, on the edge of the graveyard and between two lopsided box tombs, I could see two figures. One looked to be a lanky man in a heavy coat, the other a blonde woman waving her arms, scarf flapping madly in the air, from her stance arguing loudly but the wind stealing her words. I couldn't recognise either of them from that distance, but the evident tone of the argument disturbed me on a deep level. Man versus woman has always ended badly for me, so I stood and sent her positive vibes while I watched whatever relationship drama was being acted out above me while also watching my grandchildren.

I looked back at the children, then back up the cliffs, and in that instant of inattention the couple had gone.

Chapter 2

We All Fall Down

"ICE CREAM, NANA," yelled Myha. A demand, not a request.

"Brrr. Too cold for ice cream." I gave an exaggerated shiver. "I can see ice in the mud ripples over there."

"Yes, ice cream's for any weather," Minnie joined in, then Collin ran up and grabbed my hand.

"You taught us that, Nan," he said with his cheeky grin. "Ice cream, ice cream, we'll all scream for ice cream," he carried on, and I was soon being dragged to the steps and pushed up playfully by children chanting, "Ice cream, ice cream, Nan wants some ice cream."

I will get so fat. What's that? I don't have to eat it, you say? But that's torture, keen and true. If they eat ice cream, so do I!

⸺

As we came out of the newsagent's, licking ice cream cones, a woman with no coat on despite the temperature, was marching down the path on the other side of the road. Arms and scarf hugged around her to ward off the chill, face red with cold, or fury, her usually neat blonde hair lank from windy salt air, red painted nails flared against the grey of the world as she swiped a hand across her nose. She was the woman from the cliff top. Now I recognised her: the local publican's wife—Lisa Gilroy.

But she had passed on by, not noticing or not caring that I was staring at her with this huge need blossoming in me, an almost overwhelming desire to run over the road and take her in my comforting arms and get her to spill all her worries to me.

I fought it down. I can't cure everyone's emotional ills; look how much it took to 'fix' mine.

I gathered up my wards and went home, trying to push Lisa from my mind, trying to concentrate on house duties and homework to do and dinner to get, but how I wished I had gone to her then. How I wished it later.

⌇

That evening, someone hammered on the front door and rang the doorbell too for good measure. I hurried to the peephole and saw Lisa Gilroy's husband, Terry, standing agitated under the outside light. He's a tall chap, and as he stood there in his long coat he had rather the shape of the person Lisa had been arguing with on the cliff top. 'Suspicious much?' I thought.

Even as I opened the door he was saying, "Have you seen my Lisa, by any chance? I can't find her anywhere and I'm getting a wee bit worried, like." Gavin arrived before I could answer and Terry went on hopefully, "You seen her, Gav, mate? Getting right worried, I am now. Not answering her phone, neither."

"Last time I saw her she was in the pub wit you," Gavin said.

"Invite him in, you two!" Vana said from behind us. "Bozhe mir; it's freezing with the door open."

"No, no, I gotta get off, thanks," Terry said, and I wondered why I was stalling. If I admitted in front of Gavin that I'd seen them arguing, Terry might be very embarrassed, but that wasn't the point. I had seen her fine and well after that cliff top debacle, hadn't I?

So Terry was walking smartly up the path as my slow clockwork brain finally worked through a way to answer and I called, "I remember now. I saw her walking in Church Street towards the pub at 4:15."

He span. "What? That's like four hours ago. I'm going to coppers," he declared and ran off, literally chuffing off into the darkness of the unlit road.

I told Gavin what I had actually seen. "I didn't think Terry needed to know he'd been seen arguing with his wife. He might think I'd spread it all over."

"Now, now, Mother," Gavin said in an unwarranted weary voice. "Remember my rule. No adventures here at the seaside."

"Pft. Was hardly an adventure last time, was it," I retorted. "Nearly died." And a nasty memory flared in me so suddenly that tears welled in my eyes, and Gavin held me until I had pushed down the ghastly thoughts in the way the Witness Programme psychologist had advised me, and all was peacefully hidden inside me again.

☙

Once I had dropped off the children at school the next morning, I made my way to The Smuggler's Joy pub, which is set on a slightly hillier part of the land, far enough back to not feel the effects of the slipping cliffs that ate the other pub some years back. The Joy overlooks the sea, the beer garden one of our attractions in the summer with a huge tent-like covered area shielding customers from the sea air while affording them glorious views.

Fellow pensioner and grandma, June Bailey, intercepted me at the end of the road and we walked together. June was the first person in Kerton to befriend me, then came others, but June was undoubtedly my best friend, something I had not had since high school. I had found a need to fit in, to be wanted, and with my family's rather waning interest in me June had kept me afloat with her humour many times.

Other than that she believed in fortune telling and the afterlife spirits guiding us, things I had little faith in, she was a perfectly perfect friend.

"Have you heard?" she said, with all the excitement of a gossiping Gerty. "Lisa Gilroy's missing."

"Yes, Terry came round last night looking for her," I said. "So, no luck, poor man. I know what it's like when someone vanishes and you don't know where they are."

"Police were there last night," she said, indicating the pub we were approaching. "I gather they went all over the cliffs."

"That sounds like they fell off the cliffs."

She tittered. "You know what I mean."

"I expect they'll be coming to see me soon, then."

"Why?"

I told her I'd seen Lisa walking up the road with no coat, looking angry.

"Ooh." Her face lit up at the idea of scandal. "Wonder if the little lady had an illicit boyfriend and she broke it off and he's really broken it off with her, final-like." She opened her eyes wide. "You know what I mean."

As we reached the Smuggler's Joy car park, I stopped and stared at her in a deprecating way.

"Honestly, June, I wish I hadn't told you. What a horrible thing to surmise from so few clues."

"Hmpf." She adjusted her fur hat and plumped up the red scarf around her neck. "Wouldn't be the first murder round here," she said tartly. "Human nature, isn't it?"

"You should ask the spirits where Lisa is."

"Spirits only speak when they want to," she said, "and well you know it."

"I only know what you tell me."

She gave a hesitant laugh and fidgeted. "So, you want I should ask my cards if Terry had anything to do with Lisa's disappearance?"

"I was thinking more along the lines of just asking where she is, but yes, why not? Give it a go."

I had become distracted by the sight of a police car outside the pub and was looking across at it.

"Hmpf, I can tell you're not listening to me," she said, following my line of sight. "Police cars more interesting, are they? Oh well, I could give the crystal ball a go, I suppose. No harm in asking."

As we stood there talking, a policeman exited the private gate of the pub—the gate that leads to the publican's back door—and he stopped to look across at us. He stood there and, as I looked over at him, I realised with a start he was gazing at me, rubbing his chin and frowning.

I excused myself from the curious June and hurried over before he let the cat out of the bag by using my old name. She stood and watched.

My hair is no longer so short and pink hued, I have garnered another year's worth of wrinkles and even bought different glasses, but Sergeant Williams was a proper copper and had recognised me nonetheless.

"Fancy seeing you here, Sergeant Williams." I smiled as I met up with him. "Oh, hang on, you didn't get shunted to a lower dominion on my account, I hope?"

"Not at all. Transferred to Poole on account of the mother-in-law's problems. Nice to see you!" He beamed, shaking my hand avidly like he'd just met a screen star he followed. His voice went lower as he leaned in. "Errr…what name you going by now? Don't worry; know all about the Hartpury case. Knew you'd been moved off somewhere for safety, didn't know it was here, though."

"Molly Smith. Has no charm to it." I smiled ruefully.

"Ahh, so, are you the Mrs Smith I'm s'posed to be interviewing in the case of the missing Mrs Gilroy?" he said, suddenly all unsmiling. Though, to be fair, a missing woman is as unsmiling a thing as you can find.

"Yes. Look, can we go inside? It's bloomin' freezing out here and my friend stood staring at us over there will assume we're having an affair, if I know her."

We sat ourselves in the snug where the wood-fire was blazing, and I told Sergeant Williams what I had witnessed on the cliffs and in the street, not that my wobbly descriptions were much help.

I didn't add that I thought the man arguing with her might've been her own husband. It would be too embarrassing if I was wrong. When it was all over we said our goodbyes and I left, hoping Lisa would turn up soon.

That afternoon the children dragged me down to the beach as usual. It was fine and bright with ice in the air—bracing, as the walkers like to say. I strolled backwards and forwards, looking for any interesting things in the sand or the flotsam that collects after each tide, skimming rocks into the grey-scummed sea while the twins remade their washed away castle in the same place as the day before and the day before that, and Collin found them new pebbles for the windows and steps, running backwards and forwards like a maniac.

I think they all have Gavin's mindset of don't do anything unless you have to, unless you are nagged to. I thought it was just teenage boys who got like that, but Myha and Minnie at just six tender years were terrible to control. No, I don't mean control, I mean to care for, to point in the right direction, to offer help to. Or maybe I was just lousy with children other than as a watch dog, or is it I am just too old in the generation sense? Aeons have passed since I had my own child to care for and the rules have changed like a continental shift.

Collin loves to mock my non-expertise on the PC, though he lets me play on shared games sometimes, and I am writing my memoires in Word, little by little, as I fight through painful remembrances of my last home.

I have a mobile now in case of problems, but every time I look at it I am reminded of the picture on my lounge wall: a pair of boots sticking upside down out of the mud, the only picture I have of a man I befriended, who helped me… Hugo.

I must stop thinking backwards. Positives: food really does taste better when it's eaten sitting on the sand, out of the wind, on a not-raining day. Summer days are glorious, the views over the sea are spectacular, the neighbours are nice and there's not much litter until the tourists start to arrive.

"Nan!" came Collin's shout from down the beach, enough anxiety in it to make my heart sink. "Come look what I found."

I glanced back at the sand-playing twins, then hurried to where Collin stood, agitated, farther along the beach than he was allowed to be, at the base of some slippage, all rocks and mud and sand slumped down off the friable cliffs like a sloughed skin. There used to be smuggler's tunnels in the cliffs, hence the name of the pub, but falls had covered them all.

"Be careful," I said looking at the high slumps in concern. "Your father would whip me if anything happened to you. Go back up with your sisters now; scoot."

"But, Nan," he whined, "look there." He pointed to something in the pile and my heart jumped.

A hand, slim, white, with red painted nails, was lolling out of the mud bank.

Chapter 3

Bang Bang

COLLIN'S WIDE EYES were fixed on his find, and he seemed to be panting, nervous breath clouds condensing around his head like mist. I stretched and leaned and prodded the pale hand with one gloved finger.

"Plastic," I lied glibly. "A mannequin. You know, a shop model sort of thing. I'll call the council; get them to shift it so no old ladies have heart attacks."

He looked at me and I saw doubt on his face, but he shrugged and ran back up the beach so I took out my mobile and dialled the emergency number.

When it was promptly answered, shielding both the microphone and my mouth from the wind, I said in a voice trembling with nervous tension, "Hello. I just found a body under Church Cliff."

⁓

Gavin and Vana were not happy to come home and find a police car outside the house.

"Dad, Mum!" Collin yelled happily, running to them the moment the front door opened. "I found a body, a real live body on the beach."

Vana must have taken him to another room, as only Gavin came into the lounge where I sat with two policemen; Sergeant Williams and another chap, so young and fresh-faced I'd have taken him for a schoolboy.

"Mum," Gavin said with a frown and a voice that implied I was the naughty child, "what did you do now?"

"I didn't do anything on purpose," I said indignantly. "Collin found a body on the beach. Likely, poor Lisa Gilroy."

Gavin sort of nodded a 'Hello' to the policemen before he asked me stonily, "And how much did my son see of this body?"

I stuck my nose in the air. "Honestly! Don't fret so. Only her poor white hand was sticking out of the mud fall, and I told him it was plastic. It's not like we danced on her bloodied corpse, is it?"

Sergeant Williams, used to seeing bad things, I would have imagined, reassured the still unhappy Gavin. "She was almost entirely covered by a recent landslip, so quite possibly the fall killed her, but we'll know more after the autopsy." He stood up. "We'll mosey off now, Ms Smith; thanks for your help." He nodded goodbye to Gavin and the policemen left.

Seconds later I had Gavin on my back. "It's attracted to you, isn't it, Mum? You're like a magnet to trouble."

"Don't be silly. Don't be nasty. It's like the man said, Collin only saw a hand. Why such a fuss?"

"I don't want my kids involved in anything."

"Who's involving them? I told Collin I thought it was a mannequin's hand, got him away from it, called the police then brought the children home and they were oblivious until that silly policeman mentioned 'body' on the doorstep."

"What?" said Collin's voice as he came in, eyes alight with childish fervour. "You can tell me about bodies, you don't have to lie, Dad, I'm a big boy."

"You're eight, Collin. That's too young to be seeing bodies."

He shrugged. "I do look on the Internet, you know. There are hundreds of kids living in places at war. I've seen—"

"Maybe not so much Internet," Vana said as she came in, frowning.

"You can't hold back information from them," I complained. "Children need to learn. Their brains are like sponges, soaking up information, or so I read on the net."

Vana folded her arms and challenged me. "And when he gets around to the nasty stuff?"

"You can't control children, only what they read, and even that control's wrong in its own way. They need to know the bad as well as the good to make up their own minds."

"Not about dead bodies at eight," Vana snapped.

"Then when?" I asked.

"I am not having this conversation," she said, "with an old lady who half the time can't remember her own name! Rocky," she wheedled, using her pet name for Gavin like a bargaining tool, "this is your family. You tell her how it goes."

Gavin sighed. Vana realised she'd lost the battle and stormed out, almost slamming the door behind her.

"I think you're a bit too liberal, Mum," Gavin said.

"Oh really," I said, the words copiously laced with sarcasm. "So maybe, if I am so dangerous, such a magnet to trouble suddenly after the last year's peace and quiet, I'd better go find somewhere else to live before aliens come down and abduct us all." I stalked out.

"What we need," Gavin's tenor voice boomed from behind me, "is a family discussion, not a bloody mass walk out!"

But as his angry cry faded I was already in the connecting corridor and reaching for my flat's door handle. Misty, my calico cat, asleep on my sofa as usual, stretched and yawned when she saw me, showing all her sharp little cat teeth. I wanted to borrow them and bite Vana but, being civilised, I chose to sit and stroke Misty, one of the few constants in my life, who promptly asked to go out.

I should pack up and go; go somewhere, I don't know where. But despite everyone having issues with me, I could be mature and deal with it. I really had no authority to say how the children were to be raised. I was basically their guardian, their cook, their escort to and from school, a helper with homework, plaster-bearer ready for scratches.

Reviewing that list in my mind I could see my value to the Smiths. And I didn't forget things as much as I used to. The constant activity seemed to help my memory. Vana was just being Vana.

If I were to leave, how complicated their lives would be, reverting to the chaos and juggling they'd had before I'd arrived. Vana would have to give up her job again as she'd never find a minder who did all I had done for them—not at my low price of, oh yes, free. I was surprised she was even risking chasing me off. I expect she assumed I wanted to rest in this comfortable yet well-earned bed forever, so I wouldn't walk.

I sighed in discontent and went out to the balcony and the testing early evening sea breeze. I had adored that little balcony from the moment I had first seen it. Yet, that time, as I gazed out on the darkening view, in a strange twist of the mind, I looked across the grey mass of the sea lit only by a few lights from the town and a half moon, and I saw instead the fields of Hartpury. Life, eh? Homesickness: the last thing you can control.

It was time for the children to go to bed, so I went to that task from force of habit, feeling love for the children but speaking politely and tersely to my son and his wife when I encountered them in the kitchen, then I made sure Misty was back in for the night and went to bed after my cocoa and fell asleep quickly, slipping into a bad dream of dark wells and wet faces.

After the school drop-off the next morning, I decided I ought to go see Terry Gilroy, offer condolences or something. I knew from past experience that the bereaved often need someone to talk to but won't admit to it; especially men, who thought they had to be big and tough and hide their emotions.

The pub's front door was shut, of course. It only opened for business from 11AM onwards normally, and I wouldn't have been surprised to find a note on the door saying 'Closed until further notice due to bereavement', or something like that. So the chances were that he was still in bed or on the phone. I remembered how much sorting out I'd had to do when my own husband had died a few years before. Perhaps I was remiss in coming there. He more than likely would have neither the time nor the inclination to see me.

In the quiet-for-tourists months, some repairs were being done to the main doorway's porch, a pile of cut white stones neatly stacked by the half dismantled archway, and a small skip of rubble on the other side. As I walked into the car park and along the side of the building to see if I could see anyone moving through the kitchen window—yes, I am that nosey—an off-white Clio with a chugging exhaust drove into the car park. No luck here, sir; no beer today, or did you come to pay respects?

I was looking at the budding bushes around the car park, wishing them to bloom and give some colour to the place, when I heard the car door open and shut and a tall, thin and heavy-coated man called over, startling me, his scarf obscuring his ruddy cheeks as he said, "'Ullo, love, you know if anyone's home?"

"I don't know," I said. "It's not normally open until 11 anyway and there's a problem in the family."

He nodded, giving me a long measuring look, and I half expected him to say, 'Here, I know you, don't I?' but he wandered off as I turned around the corner of the kitchen extension to face the cold sea view. The wind—oh, that blasted eternal wind. I adore the summer days and nights; hate any other season.

Litter, a crisp bag, rustled and scurried away from me like a dry leaf. I leaned over and grabbed it before it escaped, thinking: note to self, petition the town council for more lidded bins.

A sudden wheep wheep wheep and the pub's alarm was going off. I hurried around the front of the building to see the be-scarved man carrying a sack of knobbly somethings, emerging from the private gate. "Wasn't me," he said in strange apology as he spotted me. "It just went off."

I shrugged; maybe time for me to shift too before I got the blame for something.

The alarm shut off into blissful silence, then Terry Gilroy, dressed only in plaid pyjamas, rampaged out of the private gate yelling, "Stop, thief!" at the man now starting up the Clio and, as the moving car's window wound down, he was pointing a revolver at Terry.

I turned tail and hastily scurried up the earthen bank of the footpath, hiding myself in the bushes while the shots I had expected to hear never happened but dull whangs came instead. I peeked out and saw in admiration that the bold Terry was pelting the car with stones from the skip while the car attempted a very feeble twenty-three point turn to get away with much yelling and cussing emanating from within it.

A half-brick impacted the windscreen and a hole appeared. The driver stalled in shock and fired the pistol. And Terry, still bombarding the car with stones as fast as he could, staggered, blood appearing on his upper arm, falling to his knees as the car drove off with its shattered window and pummelled paintwork like it had been caught in a meteor shower, and I hurried to Terry while calling emergency services for the second time in two days.

Gavin would have a fit over this.

Then I thought of how the driver had looked at me. What if he'd recognised me? How much worse could the day become?

Gavin would have a double fit if I was silly enough to mention that.

Chapter 4

Nice Men

"SHE WAS MURDERED," Terry's cracking voice said as I crouched beside him in the car park and wrapped my scarf around his bleeding arm.

"My Lisa," he said bitterly, eyes damp, lips trembling. "They murdered her."

"Who's they?" I asked the bereft man sitting in the open on a cold day wearing only his PJs. He started to shake, from cold or shock or both.

"Oh," he said sadly with a tiny huff of black amusement. "That's a tale and a half, that is, Molly. You don't wanna know."

And I really, really didn't.

Well, yes, actually; I did.

I managed to get him up and helped him round the back of the pub and in through the private door, until he sagged onto a bench in the snug and I took off my coat to place it around his shaking shoulders.

I unlocked the front door for ease of access for the ambulance crew then listened to Terry's sad tale while we waited. I heard how Lisa had been trying IVF, and failing, and failing again, and she'd sold all her jewellery and all their savings were gone and it had run to the point where she was ruining the future of the pub. He'd backed her up as much as he could, but then she'd really got herself into trouble by borrowing money from a loan shark—which he'd not known about until too late.

He sounded such a nice considerate man that I could have wept for him.

"Terry, if you've got nothing valuable left, what did the man who shot you take?"

"Well that there mad woman, the one she borrowed money from, she wanted the money repaid, you know? The only things we had left of value were a few old collectors' dolls, but Lisa wouldn't sell them, you see, said they were her dollies, like her babbies, and we had to keep them for the kiddies, for the future." His lips trembled. "What future now, eh?"

I waited in silence while he composed himself, listening for the distant sounds of a siren. "But the mad lady had said she wanted 'em," he went on. "Wanted the Sasha dolls from the 60s and the German bisque-headed things that looked like Chucky to me, and I guess an argument broke out. Sal had been bashed about the 'ead before she was chucked over, the coppers said." He suddenly broke into huge man sobs and I patted his back like he was a great big baby, not knowing what more I could do.

He sniffed and wiped his nose on my coat. To be fair, he was in a state so had probably forgotten

37

it was my coat. It has a lot of dire stuff from the children on it anyway. "Yeah," Terry went on, "so them dollies was only in the back room. On display shelves I made for them, for her, so the bugger got 'em easy after he'd busted the lock and triggered the alarm. Only took the time it took me to wake and get down stairs for him to snaffle the lot." He sniffed hugely.

"Okay," I reassured him, the first fluctuating wail of a siren reaching my ears. "You're doing well, Terry. You keep saying 'the mad woman', who's that?"

"I dunno. Never got her name. Sal said she just turned up, said she'd heard she wanted to borrow some money and she could arrange it, and my Sal dealt with her, but she had these eyes, Molly... piercing dark eyes, like she was going to kill you just by looking at you. Course, with eyes like that I wouldna trusted her from the get-go. But Sal, nah, she wouldn't have listened to me." Tears rolled down his cheeks. "I said I wanted her more than a babby, but that weren't right thing to say, apparently, so we'd had a few arguments. It were like wanting a babby was pushing us apart, and now I ha'nt got her neither." He put his head in his hands and shook it slowly. "You know, I hopes they come back, I does; come back and burn the place to the ground and all me memories with it, so I can go off and start again. Then I'll have nothing more they could take from me."

I sat there not knowing what to say, just being with him as the sirens came down the road and the ambulance swung into the car park. I left everyone to their parts in the great tragedy that is life and went home. The police knew where to find me if they wanted to talk to me… again.

&

"Lord above, Mother," Gavin said. "How do you manage it?"

I hadn't wanted to tell him, but I realised policemen turning up out of the blue to question me about the pub incident would give it away. And as for the burglar recognising me… I couldn't be sure he had, so I'd keep quiet about that.

I stuck my nose in the air. "It's not like I make these things happen. Just wrong place, wrong time."

"Just promise me this: you will not get the kids involved in anything."

"What a stu—"

"Promise!"

"Of course I promise. I will have adventures all on my own. All right? And, as much as is possible with my magnetic personality that attracts bad guys to me like moths to a flame, I will not even have any adventures. Honestly, Gavin, there I was thinking I brought you up to be a nice considerate man and now this!" I flounced out of the dining room with him no doubt glowering behind me.

⁓

June rang me that night.

"I was just consulting the spirits, asking about Lisa—and no joy on that—and Moira phoned to tell me about your exploits at the pub earlier. How come you never phoned to tell me yourself? Spoilsport. It's such fun having a dramatic friend like you. And friendly with that police officer I saw the other day?"

"Just an old acquaintance. Don't be nosey. Oh, that's your middle name, isn't it," I said a bit cattily.

She laughed then became serious. "Listen. I had a nap after dinner, and I think I got a dream message for you."

"Me? Dream message? What are you talking about?"

She exhaled heavily and the phone hissed. "I believe, even if you don't. I 'felt' it was a message for you. 'Finders keepers, losers weepers.' That was it, the voice clear as a bell, then I woke."

"It's interesting having you as a friend, too," I said. "Has it ever occurred to you that the wine talks… or the Vodka? That's a spirit, isn't it?"

"Oh, ha ha jolly ha. Don't mock my beliefs."

"I'm not. Could you ask your spirit buddies what I have to do to find a nice man?"

In the background of June's phone call a male voice began shouting for her.

"Look at that," she said in a partially amused despairing voice. "My dearly beloved can't find his golfing shoes for the morning… again. You want a nice man, Molly? I love Henry but I wouldn't call him nice. Now, I'll have to go before he has an aneurysm. Speak again soon. Ciao."

Chapter 5

Finders Keepers

HURSDAY DAWNED almost spring-like, clear skies, bright sun, fat buds on the flowering hedges, a few sheltered daffodils opening their trumpets, dandelions and daisies blooming in the verges.

Abandoning the children to the maw of the school, which they moaned about but liked really, I went to the beach on my own to plod along and listen to the gulls and the waves and hug myself against the wind trying to run off with my hat. Wrapping up warm and walking on a deserted beach in winter is an invigorating experience, I will admit. No smell is better than the salty sea air to clear your head and brainwash you into thinking life's not so bad, as long as it's not messing up your hair quality.

And there is definitely no sound in the world better than the smooth lapping of waves on the beach, jostling the pebbles into chatter, talking to each other about what has happened since they last met as rocks millennia ago.

I walked around the cliff fall where blue and white police-line-do-not-cross tape, ripped by the wind into shreds, still fluttered in the breeze. Even they couldn't tidy up behind them. I looked up to the graveyard and tried to remember what the man Lisa had been arguing with had looked like. Taller than her, short brown hair, heavy dark coat, possibly glasses, that's what I had told the police and, now it was settled in there as a firm memory, I couldn't pull anything else out of my head.

The beach gets narrower after a point. Tourist signs warn of sitting too close to the cliffs. The signs are not there for fun, I can assure you. It's a point of no return, where the slips are more likely, a place that needed a bigger, more demanding sign saying, 'do *not* walk here after a storm for a week or so until the land settles'.

I ignored the signage, of course, and walked on. And stopped.

There, around the corner, hidden by the slip, on its roof in the rocks and debris of the cliff, was the smashed up Clio from the pub burglary. 'Oh', I thought. 'Dare I look inside?' Of course I did, though it was terribly flattened. I peered in and spotted only one thing that was useful and I thought…

'One should never lose the childlike delight of finding and collecting pretty shells, or nice stones polished by ages of wave-tumbling… Or the nerve tingling excitement of taking pistols from wrecked cars.'

What had June's spirit voice said? 'Finders keepers'? Whether this was what the voice had meant or not, I felt sure the gun would be safer in my handbag than being left on the beach for someone more vulnerable to find, especially since I could see some of the chambers were still occupied.

～

After school, at the village playground, Collin was sliding in the mud, making it worse for everyone else who might want to walk that way. The ground used to be recycled rubber stuff but the council took it up when it was found to be dangerous, so now the playground's a hippo-wallow in wet weather.

Collin slid like an ice skater and landed with a whomp on the bench.

"Maybe you shouldn't do that," I said. "You'll hurt yourself, or someone else," but he went off and slid-slid-slid under the climbing frame.

"Honestly, Collin," I said as he defied my suggestions yet again. "You are a very headstrong boy. I think you will go far if you can be eased into the right direction. Anyone would think your grandfather had really been your grandfather, your behaviour is so—"

"What's that mean? Why wasn't my grandfather mine?"

45

"Because we adopted your daddy as a baby."

"You did?"

"Didn't he ever tell you? Well, I suppose he didn't have to. It's not like you were adopted."

"But if he's not my granddad then you're not my grandma and I don't have to do what you say," he crowed, jubilant at his own logic.

"Even though I am, indeed, not related to you by blood, I am still your carer and here to help."

He pursed his lips, deciding. "No. No, I won't do what you say."

He grabbed my handbag, laughing, calling to his sisters, and ran with the bag towards them as I yelled for him to stop. The girls detached themselves from the group of sensible children playing on the green top. "Myha, Mins," Collin cheered. "We don't have to do what the old lady says anymore. She's not our real nan."

"Give me back my bag," I demanded as I caught up with him. "That was very rude."

"No, this is rude," he said, the ultimate horrid little boy, and he upended the contents of my bag onto the ground as I gave a small shriek quite expecting the pistol to go off. It didn't, but Collin's smile fell abruptly. He looked up at me, then back at the pistol by his feet. The girls stepped back.

"Don't touch it," I growled. "You know it's dangerous."

"Cool," Collin said, beginning to smile. "Nan's got a gun, a real gun, super cool! Can I have it when you die?"

I rolled my eyes at him, gathered up my possessions and put them back in the bag.

"So now you know," I said with a severe look. "I am not just Nana, I am dangerous Nana, so don't mess with me, and do not ever tell your parents about what you saw, okay?" I waggled a bony finger at them, really feeling the part of the wicked witch. They nodded, tight lipped.

One up for Nana Molly, child carer extraordinaire. That might fix Collin's attitude problem.

This finder was definitely keeping.

⮑

In the night I woke sweating and shaking, the memory of that autumn in Hartpury two years ago upsetting me into a nightmare. So when June intercepted me after school drop-off the next morning, the end of the week and freedom beckoning for the two days of the weekend, and she asked why l looked so glum, I surprised myself by starting to speak and then being unable to say anything as tears rolled down my face. Sometimes you can hold it all in until the wrong question is asked, and then the flood gates open.

I went back to her house and, over several cups of well-fortified coffee, I told her what I had told so few people in my life: my PTSD problems with men; the attack at Hartpury.

From her spontaneous oohs and ahhs as the story unfolded I think she found it more entertaining than her soaps, but she was considerate and attentive.

"Why'd you not tell me all this before? I could have been holding your hand all this time," she said, handing over the tissue box when she saw how soggy my hanky was.

"As you can see, it wasn't easy to tell. I've been burying it for years. Hoping it would fade out with the counselling. I'm trying to write a book about it all, but…"

"Yes, you must. No matter how hard it seems, battle on. It'll help. Cathartic." She leaned forwards. "Is it that you're… you know, just incapable of feeling attraction? Desire?"

"Oh, it's not desire that's the problem. I have plenty of desire. Just put me in a room with some hunky male strippers."

She laughed, but was still puzzled. I drew in a great breath and leaned forwards, my hands open as if imploring understanding.

To me it was simple. If the first time you met a snake it bit you, then you're going to be scared of snakes forever, right? I was simply scared of men because the first ones had hurt me; badly.

"It's just that when a man touches me—" It always sounds so lame out loud, though. "It's like those first men all over again—like electric shocks in my system, bad ones that makes me want to run." I flopped back in the chair. "Oh God, it's impossible to explain."

Everyone on the witness protection scheme has access to a psychologist because of the traumas they might have experienced, but I felt like my clinician hadn't understood the problem either.

For a woman like June, who'd been happily married for forty years and had two sons, my warped viewpoint was probably inconceivable.

"Have you tried online dating?" she queried, showing she understood nothing.

I tutted. "I'm sorry, I wish I'd never said anything, but you did ask."

Her hand rested lightly on mine. "Molly, I'm your friend and I'm glad you feel you can confide in me."

I began to drip tears again. "June, you're the person I trust most in the world. Your friendship means so much to me."

"Aww…" She hugged me awkwardly, saying, "I love you, Molly. I want to help you. I will help you, somehow."

I managed a sad little laugh. "If you turn out to be one of the bad guys I'm never going to talk to you again."

She laughed hard. "Molly! I've been in this village since '62; ask around."

"I wasn't serious."

"You were; even if you don't realise it, you were. You've been traumatised on top of your trauma but you won't admit it.

I stared at my feet.

"Anyway," she said, "I don't think old ladies get to be what you call Big Bad Guys. We get to be NNGS, right? Nice Nutty Grans."

I laughed at her cheerful dismissal of my life's problems and thought, 'I suppose she's right. Older ladies are never BBGS, we're just their victims.'

Chapter 6

Muddy Molly

"LETTER FOR YOU, MUM," Gavin said at Saturday's breakfast after collecting the post. He held a buff envelope, turning it around and around as if the action would make it talk to him, then he frowned at me. I took the small envelope from him. It had the address right, but I was referred to as Ms Turner, my old name, my bad name, the name I would never dream of giving anyone. I looked at it in horror.

"I think you'd better burn it," I said, putting the envelope on the table and standing back as though it were a snake about to strike. "Anyone who knows where I am, shouldn't know where I am."

"You sure you told no one where you were going?" Vana asked, her porridge spoon half way to her mouth.

"No one at all, not even the postmistress so letters could be forwarded. We're incognito. That's the whole point, isn't it?"

"So," said Gavin, "it's someone from here who knows your old name."

"And that's not likely either is it?" I said. I stood and lifted the snake-letter by its tail and angled it in the light, trying to make out the blurry postmark.

"I don't know," Vana said sternly. "Is it likely? Too much sherry? Chatting to the schoolyard mums a little too much? Gossip in the shop?"

I stared at her, hardly believing my ears. "Why are you being spiteful, Vana? I never drink to tongue-loosening levels, and I'm the last person to be accused of gossiping. And, Gavin, honestly, why would anyone want to send me a letter if they live here?"

"No one is going to know until you open the bloody thing," he exclaimed.

So I opened it, butterflies filling me, and saw… "Oh…"

I wilted into my chair and handed the letter to Gavin.

His eyes ran over it. "Not good, Mum," he said and handed it to Vana in turn.

She glanced at it, drew a huge sigh, looked daggers at me and placed the letter on the table, tracing a sign on it with one finger and muttering something in her family's language. "This is what grandmother would do to remove the curse from it," she said, "but I doubt I can for you."

"I'll pack my bags," I said, sighing with resignation. "I am not sticking round here and putting you at risk. I'll book some tickets to somewhere obscure."

I went to get up but Gavin put a hand on my shoulder to stay me. "Mum, I know this is bad but

I am not letting my mother go through shit again. I'm calling the cops. Vana, you sort the kids—"

"That's what we have her for!" she complained. "C'mon, Rocky!"

"Tough; you know Mum needs help." He picked up the house phone and called the police.

"You're cursed, Molly," Vana said with no sympathy. "Accept it. My grandmother used to say once someone suffers misfortune, bad luck will always follow."

I went to my room but, back there on the breakfast table top, if you had been a fly on the wall who could read, you would have seen the words…

"Revenge will be mine. S Sanderson."

A relative of the man I had accidentally killed was after me, knew where I lived and knew how to scare me. I had no idea who they were, but I was pretty damn sure now the burglar had recognised me.

Now what could I do?

⌒

The cliff tops most likely to slip next were fenced off with expansive stretches of red danger tape. I suppose there's no point in using real fencing since in the autumn it would likely travel to join its old friends half way down the cliffs.

I stood there motionless, watching the sea, feeling age—not just mine, the age of all things, the passing of time, seeing the children growing, and then great-grandchildren if I was lucky enough, the cliffs crumbling until the sea had claimed much of the village, including Gavin's house, my flat, the pub and the little B&Bs dotted along the top road. The cliff top church was never used now due to its structural instability, the stylish village hall now licensed for civil marriages and christenings instead, until such time as finances permitted the building of a new church. Most likely sometime in the next century.

Everything would come to its end in time. But we humans like to feel, often wrongly, that we have some control over that time, build fences around ourselves with medicines, shore up the inevitable, try to live lives long and full, thinking it matters. In fact, my dying today would leave no echoes in the future of the hungry sea.

I looked back for a moment at the tall man dressed for the weather with a thick camel-coloured coat, scarf, gloves and peaked-cap with ear flaps pulled down; he followed me wherever I went. He still looked cold despite his attire; something about him was hunched. I suspected he had underestimated the wind and the way it creeps into a body.

You see, later in the day, another letter had been pushed through the letter box for my trembling fingers to open, but I needn't have worried. Inside was a police-headed missive telling me I had been appointed a custodian, which I took to mean a bodyguard.

Aware that just about anything would upset Gavin and Vana after the events of the past few days, I decided to keep quiet about the new development. Especially because, to my mind, giving me a bodyguard meant I was bait; an old lady dangling on a hook over the pool of bad guys.

The gentleman in the camel coat was Mr Quoit, my watchdog, who simply followed me around at a discreet distance. I was not supposed to talk to him, or give any indication that I knew him, but the letter had mentioned he was booked in at the Glendenning Hotel, room 6, should I need to discreetly contact him.

But I am Molly, she-who-refuses-to-act-her-age, so I couldn't resist playing with him.

I went home to get my Wellington boots, him following a fair distance back, then plodded along another path to the line of orange warning tape wrapped around metal fencing stakes, ducked under it and went slip-slidey down the first bank, looking in the sludge and crumbly clay for fossils for Collin. It's safe enough. I'd fossil hunted there before, but at that time of year and with the recent rain it was, to say the least, muddy. You had to double-check where you walked.

I glanced back. Poor Mr Quoit stood watching me from the safety of the orange line, the wind whipping at his scarf tails as he hugged himself and I didn't have to see his eyes to tell he was glaring at me.

'Will he follow me down?' I wondered, daring him psychically. I spotted some nice intact turritellids—tower shells—and reached for them, and farther over I unexpectedly saw something that would send Collin into fossil-hunter raptures and get me back into his good books: a perfect shark's tooth.

I moved over and crouched a little, wary of the mud sucking at the boots, grabbed up the prizes that lay scattered around profusely and straightened up, went to move away...

But I couldn't lift my feet. The vacuum of the super sticky mud held fast my boots.

I closed my eyes. "Stupid old woman!" I muttered to myself.

Looking up to where the ramrod straight Mr Quoit stood watching the sea in a studied display of nonchalance, I waved a hand and shouted, "Yoo hoo! Excuse me!"

His head turned and, as I lifted one foot out of the boot to demonstrate my predicament, I overbalanced, twisting sideways, landing in elbow deep mud.

As I remained immobile, fearful that any further movement would see the mud swallow me even deeper, a male voice said, "Here." He was stood a good few feet away in a mud-puddle and held one of the thin fencing stakes towards me, being too sensible a man to approach me further. Managing to get a hand out to grab it, I was inelegantly drawn out of the muddy area by Mr Quoit's pulling and my stepping out of the boots to leave the poor things behind. I plodded up the rise, following where Mr Quoit led, my socks now plastered too, feeling rather ridiculous to say the least.

Back at the top and safety, I sat down on the coarse grass—too dirty to care about getting dirtier—and said, "Thank you, and hello, I'm Molly Smith." He, of course, would know my name, but I decided to play things as though he were a stranger. The cliff area looked empty but you never knew who might be around, hiding. I decided I was paranoid, took a big breath and, as he stabbed the stake back in with its brothers—with a vehemence that perhaps showed his hidden anger at me—I went on, "I don't know what I would have done if you hadn't been there. Sunk down to Australia? I won't offer you a hand to shake."

"New Zealand," he said in a cultured voice.

"Pardon?"

He uncoiled his scarf from around his neck and I saw he was much older than I'd assumed. He had neat, short grey hair and a moustache to be proud of, and was around my age. "It is a common misconception that Australia is opposite us, when in fact New Zealand is our antipode, the land you would encounter were it possible to sink right through the Earth from England."

"So I have learned something and been rescued, lucky me." I saw his posh brogues were, like my socks, suffering muddiness incarnate, laces encrusted with gunge and mud spatter extending all the way up to his trouser's knees.

"Your poor shoes," I said contritely without really apologising. "I did make a mess of it all, didn't I?"

He didn't smile as he said, "I am Mr Quoit, as you well know, I'm sure. I've been warned what you're like. I was briefed on your capers back in Hartpury before I took on this assignment."

"Fame at last," I said, smiling in the hope that he'd smile back and magic the long, good looking face into a handsome one. "So, now we know each other, could you please escort me home?"

"With pleasure, ma'am," he said stiffly. "As long as there is no more mud along the way." We walked slowly, slopping muddily, some puzzled looks flying our way from residents, with me chatting happily to my taciturn rescuer, back through the streets and up to the back door of my flat.

Chapter 7

Playing With a Quoit

"So, I HAVE AN ACTUAL bodyguard," I said to Mr Quoit later as I sat in clean clothes in my lounge and had coffee and raisin scones. He had a fleece blanket wrapped around his waist sarong-style, while his trousers tumbled through the super-fast wash cycle with my clothes. I'd had the option to redress, so had done so, but none of Gavin's trousers were going to fit this lanky man.

"You look funny," I said, trying to make conversation to soothe his bear. "It's like you're in a dressing up parade as a poorly attired Caesar."

"Hmph. You had taken a slight diversion, you say?"

"Yes, that's right." I smiled and offered him the plate of scones. "Have another, why don't you? I made them fresh this morning."

"Appeasing me with scones, are we?"

"Well, it was just a slight diversion to collect fossils for my grandson, Collin. He's mad over them, and there's quite a good range along these cliffs, and I never really thought I'd get really stuck."

"Still an ill-conceived notion, ma'am," he said, grey eyes critical, no sign of relenting to humour. "I can appreciate the getting fossils for your grandson part, but why the risk at your age? Doesn't the local shop sell fossils garnered from these very cliffs? What if, instead of getting stuck, you had tripped and broken a hip?"

I grinned. "Because part of the value of fossils is the joy in finding them yourself, and I knew you would rescue me."

"So you have technically wasted police resources on a whim?"

"I don't know. Are you technically a police resource?"

He twitched his moustache and said officiously, "I am, madam, a retired officer of Her Majesty's Metropolitan police force. I volunteer for simple duties such as watching—"

"Ladies make fools of themselves?" I winked.

His smile was strained and polite.

"Very much so, ma'am" he agreed. "And, to be honest, though I fully understand the thrill of finding one's own fossils, a little research is called for. The Chama deposits of fine sands and silts hereabouts can produce treacherous quicksands, in which from time to time people do indeed get stuck. You see, I have been an ardent amateur geologist all my life."

"Oh! Really? How wonderful. What a coincidence," I gushed. "Would you like to see what I found in the midst of my cheery muddying, then? I managed to get them into my pocket before the er... stickage. Hang on."

I rushed to check on the washing and popped his damp trousers into the dryer on their own so they'd dry quicker. Retrieving the shells from my coat pocket, I returned to the silent, monolithic Mr Quoit to show him the ancient prizes.

He was on the settee, back to me, and my heart stopped when I entered the room and saw him with his hands in the air as if someone had a gun trained on him, but it was just Misty's contact he was avoiding. She had decided his blanket-clad thighs looked like a comfy place to sit, but he was obviously not a cat lover in the least, so he sat with his hands as far from her as possible and was too polite, or too scared, to shoo her away.

"I believe it is my turn to be rescued," he said drolly. "Cats and I have never seen eye to eye."

I removed her soft lump and put her on the floor. She ambled off. At least she hadn't hissed at him like she had with the major, the action which should have been my first warning sign that he was a ne'er-do-well.

"So you don't like cats, but are you a bird watcher?"

"No. I am a ferroequinologist."

I stared, playing the unfamiliar word through my studious brain. "Iron horse…? Ah, you're a trainspotter?"

He grimaced. "If you insist on the banality."

Not the answer I had expected, but to each his own passion.

He perused the turritellid shells with no sign of interest, but held the big shark's tooth delicately between index finger and thumb. "If I am not mistaken, ma'am," he said, "this is a fine, well-preserved specimen of Jaekelotodus trigonalis."

I blinked at the long words, and I'm usually good with such things. "Sounds like a magic spell."

He twitched a smile. "It is a tooth from an extinct species of sandshark. In these local Barton beds you could also find…" He rattled off a whole collection of scientific names.

He reached to the side table where the contents of his pockets waited, selecting a small, black police notebook with integral pencil, then carefully wrote in it the names he had spoken to me.

"So," I said, well impressed, "you know your fossils then. Collin would love to have a talk with you."

"I don't think that's advisable. I am supposed to be undercover, if you recall, ma'am."

"Molly. You must call me Molly." He looked doubtful. "Look," I pressed on, "Ma'am and Molly start with the same letter, so as your mouth forms mmm, just switch your brain mid-word to Molly. Ma... olly. See?"

"Hmm," he said, but I thought I detected a glimmer of humour. "You certainly have an interesting way of looking at things, Maolly. I suppose this means I should let you call me Stanley."

"And will you?"

He seemed to think about my question for ages, all of twenty seconds, then he decided, "Very well. You may call me Stanley in certain situations, and I believe you are sensible enough to know which circumstances I mean."

I beamed at him, a smile that was not returned although his moustache did a little jog around his upper lip, but we chatted on for a while nevertheless. He certainly had a rather officious, unsmiling manner, but I was determined to break through his shell (excuse the pun) with my charm. To be fair, I knew I'd put him on the spot a bit. He wasn't supposed to talk to me, let alone be seen or come into the house with me. 'Oh, Molly,' I berated myself, 'you really are a silly billy. You might have messed up things for Mr Quoit with his employers. Or, maybe, since he's a 'volunteer' it doesn't matter. Anyway, what's done is done. Try to behave in future.'

But I jumped straight in the deep end again. "And what does Mrs Quoit think of all this spying on people?"

"Personal protection detail, not even in the same league as spying. And Mrs Quoit..." He cleared his throat.

"Oh golly, I'm sorry, I know I tend to be a bit forward sometimes. Divorced or passed on?"

"Both, and that leaves one with..." He looked lost for a second, eyes downcast.

"A kind of regret tinged with guilt, I am guessing."

He exhaled sharply. "Regret, certainly. Very much so."

I wasn't sure if I liked Stanley or not. Although he obviously had a dry sense of humour, and a sharp wit that he wasn't ashamed to use against me, he still couldn't grace me with a smile despite appearing relaxed in my company. He was an unknown factor, and I found myself wary on the one hand and feeling a draw to his honesty on the other.

It didn't help that I was constantly reminding myself that the last man I had rather liked had turned out to be some kind of drug baron and almost killed me. I doubted Stanley was going to turn out that way; after all, he was a policeman. The man was only doing his job, keeping a safe eye on me. He might not like me at all. He might actually hate me. It might all be pretence for the sake of duty. A mindset of, if I was happy in his company I was less likely to misbehave?

I heard the children screaming somewhere deeper in their house and pulled an apologetic face, glad I was free from them that weekend.

He showed no response to the noise so I carried on questioning him. Start as you mean to go on, and go on I did. "But you know all about rocks and so on, so come on, tell me all about these cliffs and don't skip the gory details."

"They are primarily composed of unstable eroded deposits of Eocene marlstone."

"Wow, it's like you're speaking a foreign language."

"On a historical note, you know about the smugglers' caves, I presume?"

"Hence the pub's name. Yes, though I do wonder how you can have caves in such loose cliffs."

"The underlying marlstone rock was hollowed out by the sea, but it was men who added to the size of the caves by carving out the relatively soft stone to make storage spaces for their contraband. The Eocene detritus, the 'loose stuff' as you call it, gradually erodes and falls so there could be many caves hidden in those cliffs, just beyond our reach, possibly filled in, collapsed."

"Ooh… exciting. Collin would love to hear all this, though I suspect he'd get straight down there with his Dad's shovel and start digging. So, perhaps he'd better not hear."

～

A while later it was time for him to leave, dressed, smart again, shoes cleaned mainly, and trousers nice and clean. I had enjoyed his company. I remembered thinking that when I first met the major. That slightly disconsolate yearning for male companionship had filled me back then and was now creeping into me again.

As we parted company, Stanley advised me he would be having Sundays off so another chap would be taking over his duties. "Do not play with him," he cautioned.

"I would never dream of it," I said.

I let Stanley out the back door and tidied up. I was sure there would be no end of teasing or disapproval if Gavin realised I had let a man into the flat. Maybe it was because I was thinking that way and tired after my time with the mud event but, as I went to close the curtains in the kitchen, it was not my face that gazed back in the dark reflection, it was the major's. I swept the curtains across furiously. Just tiredness. That's all it is.

⁓

I had wondered how good Sunday's security replacement would be; if he would keep a little farther from me than Stanley had managed.

But I'll tell you this, he was way better than Stanley at the covert observation lark because I couldn't spot him. At all. In fact, because there were quite a few early visitors to the town—partly because of poor Lisa; murder makes for good tourism figures—I found it impossible to figure out who was watching me, so anxiety drove me home.

After a worrying while, becoming bored by midday, I began to consider if the police could have made a mistake; forgotten to send someone over and now I was extra vulnerable. I decided the best thing was to go to the Glendenning Hotel and ask Stanley, just to be on the safe side. It couldn't hurt, could it?

Chapter 8

Painting With Passion

"*H*E'S ASKED NOT TO BE disturbed," the young woman behind the reception desk said, hardly making eye contact, flicking a long skein of brown hair over her shoulder with purple-painted nails.

I'd never seen her before so I couldn't even try my wheedling cry of 'But it's just me, Molly Smith who lives in Ardeal House', and she had turned away and picked up her conjoined mobile before I had even finished speaking. And they say customer service is dead.

I was turning away when she left her post, phone still her main focus, and she moved into the little room behind the desk, so I shot up the stairs as quickly and quietly as I could. Stanley might well be tired after our jaunts, but surely he wouldn't mind my popping in to check on my own safety.

I gently knocked on the door. There was rustling from within the room then his angry voice called, "Do not disturb!"

Not put off by his tone—I'd had worse from Collin in the past few months—I knocked again. "Stanley; it's Molly. I've got a problem."

The door opened a crack and his face peered through. "Molly," he said in surprise, more surprise than I had yet seen in him. Maybe it was because he was relaxing, hair mussed and moustache awry, so I pulled an apologetic face.

"I'm so sorry, Stanley, but I'm really rather worried. Are you sure there's someone else out here to look after me, because I can't see him."

75

He almost laughed. "That's the point, Molly."

"Yes; yes, I know," I went on, embarrassed, "but you were pretty obvious and now I can't see anybody. Are you sure he didn't go to the wrong seaside or something?"

"That is highly doubtful. I briefed him myself on the phone this morning."

He gave a big sigh and opened the door a little farther so I could see clearly that he wore a paint-splattered apron over a short dark-blue dressing gown. His hairy legs showed equally hairy feet and I felt it gave him a kind of boyish charm; the innocence of a half-naked person.

"I'm painting," he said, opening the door more to show the inside of the room, waving a hand at an easel stood to one side, the canvas facing away from me so I could not see the picture. "I asked the receptionist that I not be disturbed."

"Oh, is that what the girl said. I thought she meant for me to come up. Wretched Collin's hidden my hearing aid again. Can I admire the picture?" I said, and skipped into the room before he could shut the door on me.

"No," he said firmly, moving to shield the canvas from my prying eyes.

"But I don't care what it's like," I said. "I mean, I do care. I'm sure it's good. Just a little peek, pretty please?"

"I would rather you wait until it's reached full glory," he said, "so off you go, don't worry about the watcher, and I will let you see this when I have finished. Agreed?"

I heard something then. In the silence after his words, a tiny creak issued from the wardrobe. I doubt it showed on my face that I had heard anything, and I had already mentioned that my hearing aid had gone walkies, so Stanley wouldn't realise I had heard it, but I kept my pleading smile frozen in case. His artist paraphernalia was all over the top of one cupboard, and discarded clothes were in a heap on the bed; he didn't appear to be the tidiest person when he was on his own, and he caught my critical glance at the clothes so picked them up to move them. As he lifted them, a pair of pale pink panties slipped gracefully out of the pile and fell to the floor. He grabbed them up.

"Each to their own," I said, amused.

"They are a component of the painting." His eyes jittered around in embarrassment, as if he were looking for other items he would rather I did not notice. A brassiere, maybe? "A… still life featuring underwear," he said lamely. It was odd to hear such nervousness from him. "I can assure you they are not what I wear."

"I wouldn't think any less of you if you did," I said. "A still life with underwear. That's a new one, I must admit. Quite novel. Can't wait to see it."

The wardrobe creaked again; it must have been uncomfortable in there.

Then I saw the reflection in the mirror on the small dresser, which confirmed I was certainly persona non grata. Small but clear, the image on the canvas was reflected: a naked woman, half turned away from the painter, from the waist up barely painted, but her legs and ample derrière were well executed and plainly those of a well-endowed lady.

It was only a glance, but I had seen enough, so I mumbled a contrite, "See you tomorrow," and kept up the smile as I left hurriedly.

I stopped to take some deep breaths on the landing, wondering exactly who the (probably) still naked woman in his wardrobe was and why she had felt obliged to hide. Was she a local I would recognise? I am not the kind to gossip so her identity would have been safe with me even if she were married. How embarrassing for them both. I was a git. But I still wanted to set up camp in the foyer, do some spying, see if I could catch her leaving. Tempting though the idea was, it could realistically be ages before anyone emerged. But as I stood there silently, I did hear the murmur of voices from beyond his door, and I sighed deeply, sad that I had read the situation correctly.

Then came the other noises. Noises that… you know… meant they were enjoying each other's company, so I tiptoed away, resolving to stay at home for the rest of the day.

Despite Stanley's reassurances, I was not comfortable with having a watcher I could not watch back.

Chapter 9

A Teacup Tragedy

*C*URIOSITY, JEALOUSY, a kind of lament over the hotel 'scene' built up in me for the rest of the day until I felt like a volcano about to pop, until I just had to tell someone, so I chose June, of course. Tucked safely in my bedroom that evening, I called her on the mobile.

"How absolutely wonderful," she said and I could hear the cheeky smile in her voice. "Things are really looking up for you, aren't they?"

"I just said there was a naked woman in his wardrobe and I left them having nookie, so what's good about that?"

"Oh, that bit's not good, it's your reaction that's good. You like him and that's really good."

"No, I don't," I said hastily. "Not like that."

She chuckled and the phone made the sound into a chicken clucking. "Ooh, yes you do. You're jealous; that's very good."

I managed to hold back a degree of anger at her insistence, loving phones for the fact you can silently scream and not be seen. "I've only just met him, so, no, I'm not—"

"Yes, you are. Don't argue with me, young lady. The painting was a nude, and you're envious as hell. It doesn't matter that you've only just met him."

"Hmm. I see why you need the spirit guides. You're incapable of logical reasoning off your own bat."

After another spate of chicken clucking she said, "So, what was she like, this naked lady?"

"All I saw was her bum and thigh, a bit pink and on the chunky side."

"And that really doesn't make you mad? You don't want a man to care enough to paint you that way? To have you as his muse? Girl, you're way more messed up than I thought."

I wasn't sure what her annoying questions were making me feel; awkward, exasperated, waking up something I hadn't realised I felt towards the taciturn Stanley, yet I didn't cut her off. But I did take too long to reply and she came on again with…

"You do fancy him, you minx. I know it, you know it, and you just have to admit to yourself that you fancy the pants off him. That in the end you wanted to rush into that room and drag Madam Chunky Bum off him so you—"

"God, no! You're a very odd person, June."

"I'm very empathetic. So… still life with underwear? What an excuse! Sounds like he has a reasonable sense of humour, at least."

At that I choked and laughed, but my laughter ended with a tear in my eye. I said in a more restrained voice, "Yes, okay, you win, I do like him just a little bit, but only 'cause he's the only man I know."

"Pah! Bob Elliot, Tom Heastings? Nice eligible males."

"No! Old widowers with bad breath and collapsed biceps. I do have standards, you know."

"Tell you what..." she said slowly as a plan formed in her addled brain, "I reckon I know that purple-nailed receptionist. Marissa's her name, used to work at the garage in the summer, so why don't I go and ask if she'll let me into his room when he's out?"

"What? You'd get the girl into huge trouble."

"But you got me all excited now, Molly. You can't do that and expect me to calm down quickly. Come on, he doesn't know me, I can hang around for a bit and see who comes in, or leaves; get a sneaky picture."

"No. It's his life. It's his choice. Do not go to the hotel to spy on him; promise me?"

"Spoilsport."

I said goodbye and flung myself back on the bed, true lovelorn teenager style. Life was so very cruel, bringing Stanley into my heart now, not 50 years ago when I had needed him most... not even a year ago when he would have easily defeated Major Sanderson for me. I needed a champion in my life, but I was realistic enough not to believe it was going to be Stanley, even if he was a widower with not bad breath and, from what I had seen, some pretty nice legs. And now I had discovered that I did actually quite like him, I wondered if I was going to be able to keep him. The chances were that I wasn't, since he felt obliged to hide nude women in his wardrobe. Now I got to thinking that she wasn't someone local at all, that he had actually 'paid' for her company. That was, of course, his choice to make, but I knew that kind of intimacy was something I could never give him, and my poor old heart shrivelled up again.

I was just dozing off when the mobile rang again, June all excited and bubbling with a new idea. I don't know how Henry keeps up with her zest for life. Sometimes she reminds me of me— two old(ish) ladies who gossip and plot. We should call ourselves the Wrinkly Twins.

"Let's ask the wine for guidance and have some tea," she enthused with the slightest hint of a hiccough. "I mean, ask the tea leaves and have some wine. The night is young, Henry's out with his cribbage team and I'm all alone with my bottles. Come on over, girl!"

Fifteen slightly out of breath minutes later, having moved as fast as I could in case my police watcher had gone off duty, I was taking off my coat in June's house and eyeing the white teacup and pot waiting on the dining table, which was spread with her best lace tablecloth in deference to the practice.

Tasseography, as she says it is named, is an ancient art which June has practised for many years, and she claims some success with, so despite my natural reservations I was curious as to what would show in the tea leaves.

We sat either side of the table, and she gently spooned a few tea leaves into my cup and poured hot water on them to steep for a few minutes.

"Remember," she said softly, "it's your emotions that guide the combinations. So, think about the questions you want to ask and let the universe help."

I drank the black brew contemplatively, thinking all the while about poor Lisa, Stanley-who-I-liked-too-much, and my future overall.

Then I swirled the delicate white china cup counter clockwise and upended it onto the saucer, leaving the last of the water to drain, then turned the cup back up the right way to show the pattern of tea leaves.

The ritual completed, I passed the cup to June to read. My heart missed a beat as she looked at me almost fearfully.

"Upheaval. Chaos. Death," she said quietly, "followed by heartbreak or grief."

"No, no!" I didn't want to hear what she said. "I don't believe it anyway. I was thinking of Lisa, so if anything those symbols represented her rather than me."

"Let's go again, then," she said, back to being chirpy, and poured me another cup of tea while she supped from a huge goblet of wine. "Cheers," she said. "To wine, women and righting wrongs." If she were to drink any more, I would no longer be certain if she spoke or the wine.

On her reading of the second cup, I had to give a short huff of disbelief. Lovers and deception. Unsurprisingly, they represented relationships and choices. Then the death symbol was seen. "Again?" I said dismay. "What are the odds of it coming up twice in two readings? Could it be I haven't swirled the cup enough?"

"It's definitely a coffin," June said. "Look." But as she shoved the cup and its sinister leaves towards me I recoiled. "Don't look so down," she said, her attitude still bright, but the 'predictions' weren't about her. "It's a good read as readings go. I've had some that I've had to think twice about saying. You know, your husband's having an affair, sort of thing."

"Really? Death and deception is better than affairs?" I muttered, remembering that fleeting ghost of the major's face in the window. Had he come back to haunt me? Not that I believed in ghosts any more than I did the tea leaves, or Tarot, or walking under ladders or the evil of black cats.

"Got anything else you could ask quickly?" I enquired. "A cross-reference kind of thing? To see if the projections agree."

She gave me a horrified look. "One does not play with such powers," she said stiffly.

Since, in my opinion, playing about was exactly what she was doing, and upsetting me needlessly, I asked, "How about sacrificing a chicken and reading its entrails?"

She snorted loudly. "It'd mess up my lovely tablecloth," she said pointedly, and for a second I wasn't sure if she was serious or not, but then her eyes twinkled. "Molly, accept fate is rampaging towards you no matter what I do, but getting a hint of what's to come can help you though it."

I shrugged and yawned widely. "Oh, excuse me. Time for bed. Enough excitement for one day. The children are off to the Maritime Museum with the school tomorrow, so I'll have to get up even earlier to sort them for the early coach. They exhaust me."

"Not surprised," she retorted, downing the last of her drink then looking sadly at the empty bottle. "You do too much for that family and they don't appreciate you. My lads would never ask me to look after the grandkids that much."

"You don't live with them. Anyway, that's for me to say. If I feel put upon I can assure you I have enough money saved to move on, find a new place."

"Well, have a drink of something other than tea before you go," she insisted. So after a few glasses of another of her many bottles of wine, I left her on good terms. I always do even though we don't always see eye to eye. BFF. Best friends forever, as the children say nowadays.

Walking home was not exactly nerve wracking, but there were quite a few people about that I didn't recognize and again I moved as fast as I could.

I had the gun in my bag. It lived there. Whenever I left the house I would tick off: purse, pillbox, hankie, loaded revolver. There, the essentials all in one place.

But, if pushed, could I ever use it? If my family was threatened, maybe, but I didn't want the chance to find out.

Turning the last corner to Ardeal House, I caught a whiff of scent that stopped me in my tracks and I looked around.

A couple had passed me, the woman quite tall and bundled in a thick coat, the man also tall and appearing younger by dint of his fashionable jacket, possibly her son, and I guessed it must have been his cologne I had scented; the same as the major had worn. He didn't have to be a ghost to haunt me. Never mind how much counselling I had, I would forever carry little pieces of that awful time in my head, and I was glad of the gun snug in my bag.

Chapter 10

Spying

I COLLAPSED INTO AN ARMCHAIR after the earlier than usual school run, during which I had been relieved to see Stanley from afar.

Tired already, I dropped off to sleep again, or maybe the wine from the night before was still singing in my veins. Either way, June woke me at 9AM by calling my mobile. "You won't believe what I found," she said, her voice excited and bubbling with the urgency to tell someone of her adventures.

I sat up smartly, startled into being wide awake, alarm bells ringing in my head. "What? Don't tell me you went to the hotel. I told you not to go. You promised!"

"Er, no, I don't think I did actually, but listen. I didn't need to go into his room, I had a mooch through the bins out back. Wasn't that a good idea?" She sounded like she wanted a badge for enterprise. "I saw the maid chuck stuff into them so thought I'd do a bit of bin-diving."

"Gross!"

"I only skimmed the new stuff. Had a quick shufti and guess what I found?"

"I don't know," I said, disgruntled. "Pink silk knickers?" It was bound to not be anything good. Not good for me, at least.

"I found three notes that had been started then screwed up."

"Written by Stanley? How could you possibly know that?"

"They started with 'Molly'. Who else would have written them, daftie? Come on round this morning. Henry's gone to town for a meeting…

you know, a consultation kind of thing, so more time for wine, women and righting wrongs for us."

"No, thanks, just tell me what the notes said. As if I could stop you from telling me."

"Oh, gosh yes, you'll love this, Molly."

"I will?"

"I don't know the order of them, but I'll do them in order of actio effectus."

"What?"

She drew in a sharp breath of annoyance. "Dramatic effect, you uneducated woman. Now, this one…" I heard some rustling. "This one starts 'Dear Molly': that's all it says. He must've been unsure of how to address you."

"Well, that's nice… I guess."

"Hang on, it gets better. The next one says, 'My dear Molly'."

I waited for the punch line with bated breath.

"And the third crumpled note starts… Ready for it?"

"That's what it says? 'Ready for—'"

"No, get your head out of the clouds! No, it says, 'My darling Molly'."

"You must be joking. All that from a man I only met a few days ago? You've made this all up just to get me interested in him."

"No, I haven't, you daftie! He's just been smitten with you. You don't give yourself enough credit, Molly. You may be getting… more mature… but you're still a good looking woman. And he's, you know, the strong silent type wondering how to make the first move on you."

"No." My head was spinning. "He… Oh, I don't know. I'm scared more than enchanted."

"I read a wonderful article that said men fall in love way faster than women, so that's what's happened. That's why he called you darling."

"I cannot get my head round this."

"Come over and you can see the notes for yourself."

"It makes no sense. If he's calling me darling but sleeping with his model—"

"Of course he is!" she broke in with her voice of illustrious wisdom. "He just used her as a substitute; probably called her Molly when—"

"Stop it!"

"Honestly; I don't know. You try to help a friend and this is all the gratitude I get?"

My heart was thumping. In that moment I was so angry with her assumptions I felt I would never talk to her again. But I breathed deeply and swallowed words I didn't want to say to someone who was usually my rock.

"I am grateful. And I would come on over, but Gavin and Vana are out and—"

"You can't be babysitting. What's the excuse this time?"

I don't want to see Stanley Quoit following me until these feelings settle down.

"I was going to sort the sock drawer," I said, not even convincing myself.

"Right, of course; theirs or yours?"

"There's a lot to do here, you know?"

"Oh, alright, slave. Go ahead and sort the sock drawer to your heart's content and ignore real life. I can take a hint. Pop round after school tomorrow, if you can lower yourself to my level. Meanwhile, I'm going to have a teensy tipsy alcoholic day in on my own sob sob."

"And keep away from the hotel," I said. "Promise me that. Go on, promise me properly this time. I don't trust you."

"I promise. There! What an absolutely delightful friend you are, Molly," she said in a faux scolding voice, but I imagined her smiling sneakily, and it scared me.

Chapter 11

Who's Watching?

THE SKIES WERE CLOUDY, but the clouds were at least white and high, not threatening rain. With the children safely deposited in school I was walking to June's place to see the mysterious 'Molly' notes for myself when, to my surprise, Stanley walked straight up to me from the pub's car park.

"Hello," I said smiling nervously sweet. He slipped his arm into mine in an unfamiliar yet pleasant way and darling Molly sang in my head.

I wondered why my instinct hadn't been to pull away. Maybe the counselling had been working away in my mind and I hadn't even noticed. I smiled to myself. Yes, Molly did quite like the feel of this arm around hers, but I had to ask, "Are you being weird, or is this important?"

"We have a problem," he said, turning me around so we walked back through the car park.

"I was on my way to see June," I complained.

"June?"

"Yes, my best friend, June Bailey, she only lives by the old forge. Can't this wait?"

"Visit later," he said shortly. "There's a man following you."

"Is his name Stanley Quoit?"

"Be serious, Molly. I am being serious. I saw him watching you on Saturday, my colleague spotted him yesterday and he's following us now, as we speak."

"Maybe he's just another policeman, from another department or something."

"Highly unlikely. I would have been informed of any extra help assigned. Besides, I don't think you're so important that you merit two watchers at any one point."

"Gee thanks, Honey," I drawled in an affected Southern twang. "Now ah am truly offended."

He harrumphed, which might have been his way of laughing, and we stood by the bench at the farthest end of the car park, where the breeze tickled my ears through my scarf and my knees through my slacks and made me want to walk on to escape it. Stanley appeared to be admiring the sea view, though I had to assume it was something policemany that he was doing, looking for clues on the faces of the waves.

"What does he look like, this man?" I asked, readjusting my scarf, pulling my coat closer. In a minute, if he didn't get the hint I was cold, I would walk on.

"He reminds me of Oliver Hardy."

"Of Laurel and Hardy fame?"

"Exactly. Somewhat round with a small moustache."

"All right, if he's portly, let's go on a long, long trek, all the way down the coast walk and give Mr Hardy some exercise."

"I think heading for the Cliff-Top café is in order. I am famished. Not breakfasted yet."

And what were you up to last night that kept you abed long enough to miss breakfast? No, no. He's mine now. Go away bad ideas.

We set off, his arm around mine again. I wanted to see the man following me, but I didn't dare turn and look.

"Sorry about the hotel thing," I said, as we began to walk smartly along the cliff path. "I didn't mean to be so rude and disturb your private time."

I felt his arm tense. "What do you mean?"

"Sunday private time," I said. "You doing-your-own-thing time."

"Don't mention it," he said. "The problem is past."

I wondered in whose arms he might have been that day, and why he was even holding my arm now.

And why, if he was with that nude-modelling woman, was he writing me notes with darling in them? Was June right in her assumptions?

Finally, it occurred to me that any man would likely want to hide his naked model/prostitute/whatever from the woman he... liked. I didn't want to attribute myself with any more esteem than that. There hadn't been anything romantic going on with her; he'd just been embarrassed at my incursion. Embarrassed enough to shove the poor dear into the wardrobe? I will admit the idea amused me. The note most likely was an attempt to apologise for being abrupt with me. I sighed with relief at my incredibly astute observation and looked at the arm wrapped familiarly around mine.

"Why are you holding my arm, Stanley?" I asked cheerfully. "Rather forward, isn't it?"

"I want to make it look like we are together, so that our shadow doesn't think you're an easy target."

"Why'd you have to say that!" I squeaked. "Target. Let's walk faster. I'm scared now."

"Molly, calm down. I am sorry you're scared, but I am here to watch over you. Nothing will happen to you while Stanley G Quoit is on duty."

I gave a shiver. "Right. All calmed down. What's the G for? Graham?"

"You need distracting. Try again."

I held his arm even tighter as he marched on and I guessed at his middle name, failing each time, but it was a good distraction technique. I would have to try it with the children sometime.

When we reached the cafe, some brisk walking minutes later, I sank gratefully into the seat of a double setting in the busy place. Stanley ordered an extra large breakfast platter for himself while I just asked for coffee and alternated looking out of the side window with watching the TV news on the flat screen over the serving area.

He took out his phone and sent a message to someone.

"Just checking in," he said quietly.

He had seated himself facing the door, so my back was to it, protected by the heavy rear of the padded bench 'But I could be shot in the head!' I thought with more than some alarm, and I slid down in the seat so my head was below what I imagined the line of sight from the door would be.

"What ails you?" Stanley asked, his face showing a cross between amusement and concern.

"I… Can we move? I'm scared someone's going to… you know…" I raised my finger pistol-like and tapped my head. "I feel very exposed."

"I consider that scenario highly unlikely. It is only in Hollywood that a killer would shoot someone in a cafe, in broad daylight, with so many witnesses. The beach is far more likely."

"And that's supposed to be reassuring?" I hissed. "Can't I just go hide in the flat? Have coffee and make scones while you keep guard?"

I heard the door open and saw his eyes flicker up then down.

"He just came in?" I guessed, so tense I could have broken a cup with my grip.

"Yes," he said, keeping his voice low, masking his words by shuffling the sauces and condiments on the table. "He looks a little puffed. No, don't turn to look."

"I'm happy to help him get fit. A kindness I am well known for, Geoffery."

"Incorrect. After this repast we could try going farther down the coast. Are the tides amenable, do you know?"

"You just said to keep off the beach."

"No, I said you were more likely to be attacked on the beach."

"Isn't that the same thing?"

The door bell dinged. "He's gone," Stanley said. "Likely waiting for us outside. Don't fret so, Molly. Just keep with me."

As I felt fear creeping into me again at the words 'waiting for us', Stanley's food arrived, a huge plate's worth, and he tucked in like he'd been starved for a week not just a night. I have always wondered at the ability of men to consume so much food so fast, even Collin ate at twice my speed. Vana had often complained, with only a slight measure of humour, that Gavin could empty the fridge at one sitting. Must be a man thing.

He ate steadily as I quietly sipped my coffee and gazed out of the window, hoping to get a glimpse of my follower—I felt that knowing my enemy's face might make him less scary. But although several people passed by, none of them matched Stanley's brief description.

"Gustav? Grayson? Geronimo?" I offered.

"Wrong, wrong and certainly wrong." He was smiling over his fork.

Stanley finished eating, wiped his mouth with the paper serviette, belched and apologised, then paid for the meal while I went to the ladies. On the way, I couldn't help but look outside again, and I wanted to stay there, in the safety of the cafe while Stanley went out and chased away my pursuer like a knight in shining armour.

As I returned to the table I cried, "I have it. You are Galahad, my knight!"

He steepled his fingers, looked over them and said, "No."

"Is it even English?" I asked.

"Time to go. Keep guessing. Give your mind something to worry about more than you-know-what."

But I had to give myself a firm talking to before I was ready to leave.

As we went out of the cafe's door, the sun came out from behind stacked cumulus clouds, spreading an uplifting light across the area like a monochrome picture changing into Glorious Technicolor.

In the distance the waves' tips sparkled in the new light, and for a second my spirits soared. I grabbed Stanley's arm and he looked startled.

"Are you all right?" he asked.

I smiled like the sunshine warming my face.

"Oh Stanley," I said, "can't you see? Sunshine, sea, a handsome man on my arm…"

"Hmpf," he said, but I could see the smile lurking behind that moustache.

'I am his darling,' I thought. 'He can't say it, but I know it. Is this what I have been looking for? Is he the man I have literally dreamed about?'

I laughed and leaned into him a little as we walked together down the twisty switchback footpath to the beach where we stepped over rocks and shingle to the sand. I didn't think about who was behind me, only about who was beside me, and my fear kept quiet.

"Giovanni?" I suggested.

"No, but I quite like that one."

A half hour's stiff walking on wet sand and my legs were definitely going to complain later. Stanley stopped a moment and glanced back the way we had come, then ran his eyes over the sea view in a nonchalant I-am-not-checking-on-someone-tailing-me way.

"Is he still there?" I asked. "Anyway, are we trying to lose him, Griffin? Outrun him, Gunnar? What are we doing... I can't think of any more Gs?"

"Since you are the target—"

"Stop using that word!"

"I am trying to keep you alive by keeping you at a distance from him. Where is the next path up?"

"Another mile or so." A shiver ran through me. "Why's he just watching, not doing anything? I mean, I feel safe with you, but what if he starts shooting at me or something?"

"Then we had better move faster."

"If we go up too fast, it'll be my legs that struggle," I complained as he hurried on.

"Legs or life, Molly. Your choice."

"Seriously, now. Do you really think he wants to kill me?"

"Quite likely me too, given half the chance. You wouldn't believe the characters I've come up against in my time."

After that, I couldn't talk because I was getting breathless and my heart was starting its odd beat—the one the doctor said was fine but I didn't like. It would always remind me of running from the major.

"Wait!" I said and reached into my handbag for my pillbox. Just to be on the safe side, I popped one little tablet under my tongue to dissolve. Stanley frowned but didn't ask what the pills were for.

Up the steps we went, Stanley bounding along like a man half his age. He had to keep slowing for me to catch up. I had given up his arm, not wanting to pull on it as I pushed myself, pushed my aching legs, pushed through my fear of a having a heart attack, and then we were finally back on the cliff tops and on a branching footpath wending its way through a caravan park.

We stopped. Stanley got out his phone and made a call.

"What are you doing now?" I panted, hands on knees, ashamed to be so feeble and breathless in the face of his superior fitness. At this rate no hit man was needed to get me; my own body would kill me. "Calling for a helicopter, I could hope."

"Taxi," he said and I thought it was almost the best word he'd ever uttered. "Mr Hardy will take a long time to get here and he won't know where we've gone."

"Don't forget the children," I said. "I have to be back by 3."

"How did they manage before you came to the family?"

"I don't know."

"Then they'll manage if we're a tad late. Your life or theirs?"

"Never give me that choice," I gasped, and I must have sounded cross because he fell silent.

Chapter 12

Nana's Boyfriend

W E MET THE TAXI on the other side of the caravan park and Stanley ordered it to Castlepoint Shopping Centre. I leaned back and rubbed my burning calves and thighs through my trousers. Even the children hadn't exerted me to the point of leg-aches.

Stanley used his phone, the conversation sounding like he was reporting the situation to his superiors, and the taxi shot along the bypass, past Bournemouth hospital and into the shopping centre in less than twenty minutes.

We indulged in some window shopping. He found a model train shop that I had to drag him out of, and I found a massive bookshop that he had to extract me from with promises of dinner in one of the many restaurants.

As we were leaving the shop, a rather large man barged in and for a moment I thought he was my doom as he seemed to bump into me on purpose. I gave a squeal of surprise, and Stanley put an arm around my shoulders, saying soothingly, "Don't worry. That was not anyone of consequence. Now, deep breaths, and I think it is time for sustenance."

This time I was really hungry and he smiled as I tucked into pasta formaggi. "I like a woman with a good appetite," he said, bringing to my mind the image of the rather chubby lady he'd been painting. "I was worried when you declined breakfast."

I managed a droll smile, the food not really calming my soul, only my belly.

"You never have to worry about me and food. We are good companions. Though sometimes I prefer my calorific intake in a good wine."

Thus we wandered for a couple of hours, chatting about this and that, and I jumped every time a man came close to me, whether he was fat or thin or looked like Mel Gibson, I was so on edge.

"Gibson?" I squawked.

Stanley laughed aloud, a chuckle really, but the best I had gleaned from him yet. "No," he said.

The most awkward moment was when I gave money, only some small change, to a homeless man sitting all forlorn on a faded quilt by the elevator. Stanley seemed quite contemptuous of him, so I felt obliged to lecture him on man's need to be humane to fellow man. We sat in another cafe, me with hot choc and marshmallows, and him with an espresso that had cost almost double what I had given the man in change.

As I went on about how we should be nice to each other and help where we can, an amused smile trickled over Stanley's face, his head tilting to one side, and I fully expected him to tell me I was too idealistic and out of touch with the way the world works. I know too well how it works, which is why I try to be nice to people.

When I stopped to slurp my hot choc, Stanley said, "I like you, Molly." I bit my lip, a habit when I am too excited to speak, and he put his hand around mine holding the cup on the table. I stared at it, a comforting hand, warm and strong, no scary electric shocks from it at all. "You are a good woman," he went on, and my heart melted like the marshmallows.

～

Window shopping, bad guy avoiding, and me trying to stop flirting all done, we got another taxi back to Kerton and he said goodbye at Ardeal House's gate. I was suddenly and inexplicably filled with the urge to hug him, to take that one step forward and launch myself into a world I was so unfamiliar with. But, to my utter surprise, he made the first move and leaned to kiss me, a quick peck beside my ear. I forced myself to stay still.

"Thank you for such an interesting day," he said.

"Interesting? You could call it that. I was scared, excited and full of enjoyment all at the same time. And that name guessing game, pure genius."

"I enjoyed it too, my dear."

"Stanley, you said 'my dear'."

There was the briefest of pauses. "Did I? Slip of the tongue, I'm sure. But I will put you out of your agony. I am Stanley Graham."

"But… that's what I said first— Oh, sneaky!"

He gave me a slight wink before he strolled off, and that was enough to make a not-so-old lady's heart flutter in the nicest of ways.

When I went to pick up the children and managed to talk them into going to the playground instead of the beach, I spotted Stanley come in the gate, sit on a bench, and set to fighting the breeze to read a broadsheet. "Just use the phone," I muttered to myself. "Silly man."

"Who's that?" Collin asked, picking up on my words and angle of view.

"Is he your boyfriend, Nana?" Myha asked, and all three children laughed at the absurdity of the idea.

"He's a friend. He's Mr Quoit and he knows all about rocks and fossils," I said, hoping it might get me some Brownie points with Collin. "Do you want to meet him?"

I don't think Stanley approved of my breaking his cover just for Collin, as he gave me a tilt of the judgmental eyebrow. He sat awkwardly on the bench with Collin, while the girls played with other children and other parents barely passed a glance over his presence. But, after a few minutes, I saw him drawing diagrams or pictures in his small notebook while Collin, uncharacteristically still and quiet, sat engrossed in tales of rocks and fossils. How much he understood, I had no idea, but there was no doubt he enjoyed it, his face aglow.

"Back to the beach now, Nan," Collin demanded after at least half an hour, leaping up and waving goodbye to Stanley with a great big smile. "Got some fossils to look for."

"No," I said, "we have to go home and do homework now or tea will be late."

"I want to go to the beach!"

"Who am I, Collin?"

His eyes fell, his mouth turned down. "Danger-ous Nan," he grumbled and stood placid. I wondered if I had done wrong in calling myself that, but if any mention of the weapon silenced Collin's tantrums, that was a blessing in itself.

Stanley had moved off. I wanted to yell, 'Come back. You are ten times more interesting than these children are,' but he vanished around the corner of the hall, presumably to wait until he could trail after us back home.

❧

Morning came, children bounced in, and grandmother heaved herself up to get them sorted. Vana had already left for work. Gavin was on his laptop organising something before leaving. So much for my money helping this family to have more family time.

I was feeding the children breakfast, the TV burbling in the background like it always does, when the eight o'clock news came on with its classic fanfare.

Two seconds later I was staring at the screen like an animal transfixed by headlights, unable to move.

A man and a woman had been found dead on the beach beneath Clifor's rock, a precipitous cliff a mile or so down the coast from Little Kerton. A suspected lover's tryst, the newsreader said. When the facial composites were shown I gasped into a squeaky-screamy sob that silenced everyone in the room.

The man was no one I recognised, but the woman was June.

Chapter 13

A Friend Is Forever

I T WAS ME; MY FAULT; I had done it again with my curse. The way I saw it, I had told June not to go to the hotel again, made her promise not to go, but she had gone anyway and that had got her killed. Her death was nothing to do with secret trysts or mutual suicides, she loved her Henry, and Henry adored her. I was sure of this because she had told me so many times how wonderful he was to the point where I just wanted her to shut up about her good fortune. I would bet all my money on the fact that one cannot fake nearly forty years of happy marriage when talking to a best friend.

I was sure someone had seen her poking around at the hotel, meddling somehow, discovering more than she should have about… What? What could she have discovered, uncovered, realised? Had one of the bad guys thought her a policewoman with her nosing into the business of others?

What of the mystery man who had died with her? My mind ran overtime. Could he be her killer; a man who had accosted June on the cliff top, gone to throw her over and fallen too? I couldn't imagine what she would have been doing there, anyway, a half hour's walk or more along the cliff top road.

She must have been taken there to be thrown off the highest point on the local coast.

I hoped she'd been unconscious before she fell, like Lisa Gilroy had been.

However the scenario had really played out, I was inconsolable, my tears floods, my speech gibberish, wondering how I was going to face Henry, when would the funeral be, what could I say honestly to her two sons if they spoke to me…? Such a mess of reactions. I lurked in my room, neglecting my 'duties', all my optimism gone, finding no way of awakening my usual capable self.

Gavin had to take the day off to get the children to school, then whisked me off to the doctor for an emergency appointment; he was that worried about me. But the doctor simply gave me some tablets to calm me. I doubted they could cure consuming guilt. Vana was right; everything I touched fell to ashes.

I went back to bed at 10AM, headphones on, playing strong classics, blocking out the world as words swam into my head, images of the major and the cellar and nasty things that I knew were only visiting me because of the tranquillisers, but I had no power over them. I had to pull myself together again, I had to fight again. There was S Sanderson to deal with. He was the one doing all this. It had to be him. Hadn't the police stopped him yet?

Stanley phoned me at 10:20. He'd seen Gavin take the children to school, then me driving off in the car with him and returning, and he was consequently enquiring after my health, disturbed at my non-appearance. When I thanked him for his diligent concern he managed to turn the compliment on its head. "Much of this job is about observing patterns," he said, "knowing the routines of a person so you are alerted if that pattern is disrupted."

"Ah, so if I always take the kids to school for nine and I don't show one day, you'll wonder where I am."

"Exactly what happened this morning, though seeing you with Gavin didn't trip any alarms, and I assumed you were worn out from our jaunt."

"No." I started to explain about June but couldn't finish, gabbled a sorry and hung up.

&

Later that afternoon, the door bell rang, and moments later Gavin knocked on the bedroom door before coming in with a bouquet. "Someone thought to send you flowers, Mum. I'll get a vase."

I stroked the flowers' petals, inhaled their sooth-ing scents; freesias and carnations, alstroemerias and delicate gypsophila bound in a bright, colourful bouquet not exactly appropriate for bereavement.

Spotting the gift envelope tucked down the side, I flipped it open and almost fainted.

It was printed, not handwritten, but the impact was the same as if she had written it herself.

I seem to recall this is the anniversary of the day we first had 'wine women and righting wrongs' Cheers! Many more wine-ing years to us!

She must have ordered them a couple of days prior, before she had been dragged to a cliff top and pushed over. My lovely friend, kind to the last.

On the bottom of the card it said:

"To love is to lose. But a friend is forever.
June."

By the time Gavin had returned with a vase the flowers were on the floor and I was a sobbing mound in the bed.

After that Gavin and Vana were somewhat nicer to me in my grief and let me do my own thing, though Gavin would call in or phone me every half hour, or so it seemed, to make sure I was okay. He had arranged to have as much time off as was needed—and was enjoying it, I could tell, the children cheered by having their actual father caring for them. I didn't tell them I was wandering off with Stanley. To be honest, I wanted something apart from them, someone of my own, to not feel accountable to Gavin and have to tell him everything I did every hour of the day.

It had crossed my mind that June had been mistaken for me. In a way, that made sense. To some people old ladies all look alike, and the fact she'd been at the hotel might have enforced that idea. That made me feel even more guilty, and more scared for myself, so keeping away from home might help safeguard my family, and keeping close to Stanley would safeguard me.

So I walked on the beach to meet Stanley and I had literally cried on his shoulder, and he had held me and not said a word. Nothing he could have said would have helped, to be fair; I just liked the feel of his arms around me.

That dozen or so days after June's death was a bad time, and I don't recall it all, the fogging of the tranquilisers, I suppose. I know I felt I was going crazy, in a little heavenly hell, bemoaning the loss of June's company and enjoying Stanley's.

He would update me with little comments designed, I was sure, just to calm me, to make me less frightened for myself. There was a strong criminal investigation going on in Bournemouth, he said, a bit of a fracas that he considered meant no one would be bothering with me for the while. 'For a while' was not a particularly reassuring phrase, but I didn't tell him that. In a way, I felt I'd rather the police were looking for June's murderer than worrying about me.

"Who is this S Sanderson, anyway?" I asked. Better the devil you know. "Do you have a picture of him, so I know to run the other way?"

He fished out his phone and poked and scrolled, then showed me an image of…

"A woman! I didn't expect that. Wait…" I homed in on her beady eyes. "I bet this is the woman that killed Lisa Gilroy, or ordered it done."

"Quite possibly. She is Major Sanderson's sister and, how shall I say it politely…?"

"A murderous bitch like her brother?" I offered.

"Indeed," Stanley said. "But she's busy in Bournemouth now; the focus of the investigation I mentioned, so I think you can relax a little, Molly. She'll get her comeuppance one day."

"I'll happily pull the switch," I said bitterly, and we walked on in companionable silence.

If it was damp we strolled in the weather, and if it was fine we sat on the beach blanket and watched the sea that had eaten a million souls and, along with his closeness and the medicine, it all served to get my mind back into order. I felt the bond between us strengthening as we talked, about anything that came to mind, classic trains and litter picking, the way the world was now, compared to the world of our youths, our hopes for its future, and gradually the shoulder to cry on became the arm to lean on and the hand to hold.

"The man killed alongside Mrs Bailey has been identified," Stanley said one day.

"And…?"

"Freddy Crathbourne. A small time crook, known for burglaries, did time for money laundering."

"Do you have picture of him?"

"Do you really want to see it?"

I sat on the rocks and held out my hand for his phone.

"Show me."

I looked at the mug shot on the screen. He didn't look quite the same as the artist-impression that had been shown on the TV, but I suddenly recognised him.

"This is the burglar from the pub. I'm pretty sure of it. I won't say he's the one that tipped Lisa over the cliff, though. He looks way too hefty to be that person I saw with her." I stared at his face, wishing him in hell. "June would have put up a good fight, if I know her, so I suppose she could've pulled him over with her."

"Unlikely," Stanley said. "She was struck from behind so would've known nothing about it, if that is of any comfort." He took back the phone, seated himself on the rock beside me, and stared out to sea.

"I wish I could've killed him myself," I managed to say through the lump in my throat, the pain in my heart.

"Pardon?"

"Well, what do you think? He bashed her, heaved her over, overbalanced or something, so fell with her; serves him right."

"There is no direct evidence for that."

"Stop being a policeman for a bloody minute! Sympathise with me. My best friend's been killed and I… I'm… just so shattered with all the absolute shit that's happening in my life!" I wailed and his arm came round my shoulder so I cried against him.

As I calmed, I dried my face and went on, "I'll assume Mr Freddy didn't jump voluntarily, and I really absolutely don't believe he was carrying on with June like the news said, so I say he found June snooping around the hotel and decided she was up to no good and got rid of her."

"And what was she snooping for?"

"Oh—" I had driven myself into an awkward corner. I couldn't say: She'd gone to spy on you, Stanley, and see who your muse was. "She just had this funny idea that there was something spooky going on at the hotel."

"Do ladies get odder as they get older?" he asked.

"I think we might. Bear in mind June was really into the mystic arts. She was always 'feeling' things, so who knows what she was up to."

Finders keepers, losers weepers. The words rang in my head, just as I imagined they'd rung in June's dream. I had found, she had lost.

Gulping back tears, I stood up and we walked on. Again the guilt washed over me. I had told June not to go to the hotel, made her promise not to go, told her not to be nosey about Stanley, but she'd ignored me on all fronts.

At that moment, I don't think I would have minded too much if someone had jumped out of a bush and shot me.

For Lisa's funeral, a week later, almost the entire village attended. Buried in the next town, as there was no longer a graveyard for Kerton, her plot was covered in flowers. One of the 'wreaths' was a rose teddy bear, which I found most poignant knowing how it was her efforts to get a child that had caused her death.

⌒

And the pain didn't end there, for then it was time for June's funeral. Her family had come from Taunton, so we attended the crematorium there a fortnight after her dramatic end. Henry, flanked by his two tall sons, was silent and stoic until the very last second; that awful moment when the coffin takes its final ride along the rollers into the furnace, then he had collapsed and I, among others, had gone to him and I became a wreck again consoling him.

I didn't go to her funeral reception. Not with the size of the guilt-stone hanging around my neck. Gavin drove me home and I don't think I managed three words the entire journey, then I sloped into my bedroom, put on my walking shoes and headed for the beach while calling Stanley on the mobile to begin to cheer me again.

I was in love with him. I felt it so strongly I scared myself, and when I thought of everything being over, all settled and my world safe again, I realised I would be Stanley-less again, and I felt I couldn't deal with that. Not ever.

Chapter 14

Fateful Friday

AVIN AND VANA HAD both taken a day off work and gone into Bournemouth early one Friday morning, to shop, to have some time away from nursing the old woman (I'd heard Vana say that) to be together for while, planning to be back by 6PM.

That was the ending time of the after school birthday party I had been asked to take the children to, and for afterwards Gavin and Vana had planned a film night with pizza and ice cream and I was invited.

Our village hall is a construction of great beauty. I don't know who the architect was, but he might have been into creating cathedrals before. With its high ceiling and exposed rafters, mammoth windows and curtains fit for a manor, it was the best thing in the whole village and I loved it. Its elegant curves made me happy in a way I can't describe, and the newer parts where religious symbols had been carved into the woodwork to make it more church-like for weddings and christenings and such like, had created a transcendent quality to its splendour.

And that day it was full of the beauty, and noise, and chaos, of children.

Kerton primary school is small enough that all the children tend to go to all the parties just to make up numbers. There were only six children in Myha and Minnie's class but any child would whine it was no fun having a party with just six children and get their parents to invite the whole school. This, from the screaming horde that met us as we walked in, appeared to be exactly what the birthday girl, Dani Weaver, had done. Thus did I discover that forty excited children have the sound-load of a crowd of four hundred.

With the thumping disco music, the gaily coloured balloons that floated all over like giant soap bubbles, the decorations hanging from the beams and the big birthday banners, it looked to be a splendid event. I had my eye on the tables, piled high with tablecloth-covered food. I hoped they had my favourite: egg sandwiches. It's for the children, I reminded myself, not that that would stop me from snaffling some.

Stanley had tagged along to the hall with me, perhaps to watch out for children who might be hit-men in disguise, as he wasn't the most cheerful party goer I'd ever seen. He was very much on edge that day and, even when I leaned against the wall and watched the games with him and tolerated the loud dance music, he hardly smiled.

"I love this place," I said above the music. "Don't you think it's divine; the construction, the workmanship? It's one of the best buildings in the village; one of my favourite things."

There came no reply, though his eyes did look up and around so I knew he'd heard me.

I was getting used to his quiet times, to be honest. Better a man who knew when to open his mouth, than one who talks on and on about nothing. I was aware he knew something of my past life from police records and, although he had told me of some of the adventures of his life, he had never mentioned his deceased wife or any children. I began to wonder within his silence if he might have children he missed. He could have lost a child, and the party brought back bad memories.

You know me; I had to inquire. "Do you have children?" I asked into the beat that made me want to move my feet.

"Never had the fortune," he replied. "My wife hated the idea. Nowadays, I prefer snakes. Frankly, I see little difference in the two species."

I almost choked. Oh dear. I should have asked sooner. The children were an essential part of my life. It wouldn't do to have a partner who—

Oops, I was thinking too far ahead.

"I'm sorry that happened to you," I said, really meaning it. I could not have imagined a life without children, hence our adoption of Gavin. "Children can be vile, that is true. I have to agree on that, but they are also adorable if they're your own."

He looked at me askance and arched an eyebrow with a look of are-you-sure?

"Oh come on, you enjoyed talking to Collin about the rocks and things, didn't you?"

He managed a begrudging nod. "Grandchildren," he murmured. "Something I could never envisage."

"So, do you keep snakes? Who's looking after them while you're looking after me?"

"A good neighbour."

"Could I see them sometime? I actually love snakes."

I felt the hesitation.

"I suppose," I said cautiously, lowering my voice in a quieter moment, "that when this is over, this watching me thing, you have to go home and leave me here and I will never see you again."

He didn't reply but his lips pursed with deep thought.

I watched the happily milling, chatting and excited children, and their excitement filled me too, so I leaned a little more his way to say, "You could stay, you know."

"Stay?"

"I mean, I'd like you to stay. Wouldn't you? The flat's big eno—"

He abruptly pulled away from me and vanished out of the swing doors that separated hall from corridor. Had the question really been too forward? I sighed. We'd been getting on so well it seemed, to me, to be the perfect next step in our relationship. There's not time enough for any of us to wait for the right moment. I'd had to jump in and ask or spend the rest of my life wishing that I had.

But I was kidding myself, wasn't I? Stanley was into thick-thighed women, and a sexless marriage would not be his idea of heaven.

I was about to follow him out when the lights dimmed and the doors swung open at the ceremonious entry of Moira Weaver carrying the birthday cake, all the bright little cake candles flickering upon it, counting up a child's life, symbols of hope for Dani's future. I wished her well.

I found Stanley in the kitchen. With his back to me, he leaned on the kitchen counter, talking to Dani's father, Nigel, both men with beer glasses in their hands. Beer trumps Molly, I realised.

"Time's up, gents. Your lady friend's hunted you down, Stan," Nigel said with an amused grin, raising his half-pint to indicate me in the doorway. "Don't you be blaming him, ma'am, it's a tad noisy in there."

"Doesn't worry me in the least," I said. "Happy to see him having a good time."

"Ooh, nice attitude," Nigel said. "Got yourself a keeper there, Stan-my-man." He winked.

"I'm just going out for a breather," I said. "My beer-less way of relieving my ears."

Outside the door I found myself laughing inside: Lady friend. Was that how Stanley had introduced me in my absence? How sweet. I liked it.

Now, wouldn't duty oblige him to follow me out?

As expected, the hall's door swung open and Stanley emerged. He pulled his coat around him and glanced at the clear sky. "Frost again later," he said.

"I do wonder if summer will ever come. It feels like it's been winter for the past six months."

I breathed deeply. The air was pleasant, in the distance the waves sang on the rocks, it was all peaceful.

"Molly…" He coughed as if he had something hard to say and stepped up to me. "I have… in there… when you asked… I'm sorry I dashed out. I was quite fazed by what you were saying about the flat being big enough—"

"Oh no, no." I twisted away in embarrassment then turned back. "I didn't mean to discomfit you. Umm… think nothing of it. Just a lady looking for her last… something or other. Now you've got me all tongue tied."

"Nigel, the gentleman in the kitchen just now, he gave me a few pointers. I am too old for this game so I will just say…" He gave a meaningful hesitation. "Could we make this work?"

"What?" On paper the word looks little, but it was expelled from me forcefully enough to blow a metaphorical hole in the page.

I looked at him, he looked at me, and for few trance-like minutes both of us were unsure what should come next.

He raised a hand to my cheek. "Should I kiss you?"

"I don't know," trembled my voice. "This simple touch is bold new ground for me."

"I do know what you mean. In all sincerity I do. I have read all your files now."

I started to cry; from happiness for a change, but then I remembered the painting, the sounds I had heard from that room, and wondered if he truly understood what he would be losing in a relationship with me. "Do you really understand my problem? Do you know what you're letting yourself in for?"

"Molly, it's your soul I'm after, not your body."

I found myself taking huge gulps of cold air to calm myself.

"Molly?"

"Oh Stanley, do we have a lot to sort out!"

"If the flat is unsuitable, we could buy Chapel Cottage."

"Did I tell you I fancied that house? Reminds me of the one in Hartpury. The one the major's idiots burned down. Oh, now you've done it you've got me all excited and I won't be able to stop talking—"

"Sssh…" He put a finger to my lips. A shiver of anticipation ran through me, but he took it to mean I was cold and opened his coat to wrap it around us both.

"So," he murmured against my head. "Are you happy?"

"Oh yes," I sighed, listening to his steady heartbeat. "Happier than I ever imagined I could be. I just wish June were here to see this."

"Then my job is done," he said.

Only later did I find out what he meant.

❧

Party over, egg sandwiches successfully snaffled—along with some birthday cake—the children rushed out, and I went to get my coat. Coming out,

I could see neither my grandchildren nor Stanley, not that I was too worried. Ardeal House was but a few minutes' walk away, and Stanley had also gone, so was likely with them. We had an announcement for the family, so it was apt that he should take them home. I smiled. What a day!

Marion Weaver exited the hall and locked the door behind her.

"Have you seen my three?" I asked. "Lost sight of them in the crush."

"That man friend of yours took them off," she said. "Nige said he seemed a nice chap." Her eyes sparkled with feminine glee. "Nige says he told him to— Oh."

She stopped, probably suddenly realising Stanley might not have taken her husband's advice and she'd be putting her foot in it.

"Get real and propose?" I suggested with a slight smile.

"Did he?" she asked, eyes wide. "Oh, come on, Molly, do tell."

I shrugged. "After a fashion. He's not that good with romantic stuff."

"Show me a man who is!"

"Funny he took the kids off without waiting for me, oh well, Collin knows where the spare key is, so they can get in okay."

Marion congratulated me and went off. I wouldn't have to tell anyone about my new relationship. It'd be all over the town by the next week.

Gavin's car pulled into the car park. I was itching to give them my good news, but my excitement waned as I saw Vana and him looking around, puzzled, then Vana jumped out of the car and marched up to me. "Molly, where are my children?" she demanded. "Tell me you haven't mislaid them!"

"God, Vana, get off my back, will you? I have never lost the children. Why do you have to be so mean? A friend took them back to the house."

"We just came from the house," she said, stone-faced. "We didn't pass them on the way."

"Oh…" I panicked a little. "Maybe they… they went down by the cross roads."

She said something foreign and angry, gave me the 'look' and hurried off with Gavin. I felt a real stab of anger. I kept thinking Vana and I could weather the storm of my settling in, mother-in-law versus headstrong daughter-in-law, but here it was being laid bare again. It was a shame their trip to town hadn't lasted longer or they could have just come home and the children would have been bathed and ready for film night, and bursting full of stories of the party.

Gavin would likely be angry enough to get home and find them in the care of an undercover policeman. A policeman who could become Gavin's stepfather. I laughed at that idea.

Families!

Smoke hit my nose. An inconsiderate bonfire to ruin the lovely evening?

I looked around for the culprit and through the windows of the hall kitchen, I saw flames.

No!

At least this couldn't be my fault, though I couldn't imagine what had started it. I hurriedly called the emergency services, asked for the fire brigade, watched as the blaze ran amok, lapping up the curtains, smoke filling the rooms I could see into, red flames trickling up walls. I stood way back, the horrid hypnosis of the fire affecting me, making me stand trembling with stress. This was not the way I wanted to remember the day Stanley had proposed.

Passing cars stopped; people asked if the fire brigade had been called. I couldn't do anything more so I hurried home full of painful remembrance of my little cottage in Hartpury going up in flames, and I needed to see Stanley and the family to sort out many things with them.

～

Vana leaped on me as soon as I walked through the front door and grabbed my upper arms in a forceful grip that made me recoil. "Where are they?" she demanded in the fierce and fearful voice of a haunted mother. "My kids? Where's your bloody so-called friend taken them?"

Chapter 15

A Church Of Secrets

"I DON'T KNOW WHERE the children are."
There was no escaping the fact; I had to admit it. Getting out my phone with shaking fingers I said, "I think my friend must've taken them to their place instead."

Before I could call Stanley, the phone trilled so unexpectedly that my fearful confusion made me almost drop it.

"Hello?" I said to the unknown number with Vana stood in front of me, eyes afire, hands on hips.

A deep male voice I didn't recognise said, "If you want to see the children alive, get to the church on the cliffs right now. No police or they die."

Click

"What?" Vana shouted. "I can see your face, Molly. What's happened now?"

She'd call the police, endanger her own children.

"I'm just going to get them," I said truthfully. "I know where they are."

She slapped me across the face. "Suka! You did forget them!"

"Hey!" Gavin pulled her back. "Calm down."

"If anything ever happens to them I will kill you!" she raged at me over an accusing finger.

'Overreacting much?' I thought. 'We need to have a good sit down discussion when this is all over.'

If I make it back.

I ran to my room, checked the contents of my handbag, grabbed a torch and rushed out of my own back door, thinking how the neighbours could probably hear the argument now raging between Gavin and Vana deeper in the house.

Hurrying down the darkening roads toward the cliffs, my whole body shook. Pulling my tweed coat tighter, I couldn't help but wonder where Stanley was, my quiet knight, my almost partner? He had taken the children, but now the BBGs had the children, so where was Stanley? Had they killed him? Was he captive? Was this my curse again? The fate he'd earned from consorting with me?

'You should have called the police anyway!' my inner-self argued as I sweated suddenly, hot and panicking.

'I couldn't risk that. Not at all,' my conscience agreed firmly.

Leaving voice messages for Stanley, begging him to contact me; I was in dread as I strode down the roads, a dark hint of frost in the air. I had to get the children but I needed backup. Where was the silly man? I was sure he would do his best to help—as soon as he got my messages. He was a policeman, after all. He had probably been in sticky situations before.

As I came within sight of the cliff tops I called him again; got voicemail again. "I need your help," I said in the fiercest, most despondent tone I could muster. "Someone's kidnapped the children and I can't rescue them on my own."

I looked behind me, hoping to see someone coming to help, but all I saw was the sky glowing where the burning hall and the flashing lights of the fire engine reflected on the low clouds. I heard voices calling, the lamentation of the town as one of their treasures burned. At least I was not responsible for the death of a building.

Drawing a deep breath of courage, I carried on walking to the church on my own, torch in one hand, handbag in the other, holding it as tightly as a drowning man clamps onto a piece of wood, wishing I had someone to whack with it, or the guts to use the weapon inside it.

When the bedraggled church came into view there were dull lights flickering in the stained glass windows, blessing them with a final glory soon to be gone forever. I hoped the children were okay, not too scared. I hoped Collin was regaling them with tales of fossils and giant sand sharks.

I didn't want to go in, but I had to. I didn't know if I was going to be killed on sight and the children released, or if they would kill the children too after I'd been disposed of. What kind of animal was S Sanderson? Psychopathic tendencies ran in the family, evidently.

Terror stopped my breath. My heart flip-flopped. I didn't want to get any closer. Flashbacks assailed me: the cellar, the well, the major...

And my legs got weaker and wobblier the closer I got to the building until it felt like my limbs were blades of grass. What was I walking into? Was there even the faintest glimmer of hope I'd get out? Or would I be thrown over the cliffs like June and Lisa?

As long as I can save the children.

I didn't have to worry about walking in, because in the next second the church door squeaked open and two goons, to refer to them politely, rushed out.

One grabbed the handbag I was clutching like a drowning man clutches a straw, then they both took an arm and practically lifted me off the ground to frogmarch me inside.

"Nanny!" the children yelled, tied up little souls, sitting in one of the broken box pews that were scattered about.

Two other heavies were sitting in a pew, one each side of a woman whose eyes seemed to glint in the candlelight. Getting to her feet gracefully, almost elegantly, as if she thought she was the most important person in the world, she took my handbag from the goon.

A few inches taller than me, with an unassuming middle-aged angular face, she was heavy-hipped, likely attractive once, but now with untidy short chestnut hair heavily streaked with grey, her pretty days were well over. Sporting thick drab trousers and a chunky jumper, she seemed to me a woman who wanted to hide any vestige of her femininity. And those eyes, hooded and evil and reflecting candlelight in their depths. This wasn't just S Sanderson, it was the 'man' on the cliff top

with Lisa. The woman with evil eyes, hardly rec-
ognisable as the woman in the photo Stanley had
shown me.

"Hello, nasty person," I said, polite to the end.
"Major dickhead's sister, right?"

She glared, looked in my bag and found the
pistol, took it out and angled it so the candlelight
reflected along the length of the barrel. "Freddy's old bashed up pistol," she said, almost to herself. "The one the nincompoop left in the car and
wasn't there when I sent him back for it. What did
you imagine you were going to do with it, Molly
Marshman?" She dropped the pistol back in my
bag, handed it to the goon, then took a step forward so I thought she was going to hit me and I
moved back sharply. Instead, she gave a nasty, vic-
toriously vindictive grin.

"You killed my brother," she said flatly, and a
scent wafted to me; the major's cologne. Was this
the woman of the couple I had passed in the street
on that evening after leaving June's house?

"And it couldn't have happened to a nicer guy,"
I said cheerily, "you know, what w—"

She backhanded me then, and I realised how gentle Vana's tap had been. Sanderson's strike knocked me almost off balance, my spectacles shaking on my head.

Where was Stanley? I couldn't help but wish for him to appear, and hoped he was arranging for cavalry to come charging in.

"What?" I asked, one hand to my painful cheek, "no hardy henchmen drugging me, half drowning me, messing with my life the way your brother did?"

She tilted her head to one side and malice spread on her face like hideous sunshine. "Shut up, old woman. You took the only thing I valued."

"Nothing original to say then? Full of clichés?"

"Shut up!" she screamed, ugly in her hatred, fists bunched as she appeared to resist hitting me again.

"So now you're going to say…" I battled on, talking as much as I could while letting a part of my brain try to figure out how to escape, "that you're going to take something of mine in return, am I right? Listen, everything bad started off as good. It's life that messes us around."

Her face was mocking now. "Oh my, my, my, what a little old moralising old woman you are. Did you never have any naughty fun in your teensy weensy little life of do-gooding?"

I spoke slowly, hoping the words might sink in; might affect something in her addled and distorted brain. "Revenge is a dark and lonely road. Once you go down it, there's no heading back. The question is, how far are you willing to go?"

She beamed. "All the way, of course. I want to see the look on your face when you realise what I've done; what I'm doing."

"As in?"

"You liked that building, didn't you, the hall so sleek and—"

"You set the hall alight? Pathetic woman," I sneered.

"Yes… Because you liked it." And who had told her that? "I am taking all the things you like, love, care for. Wait until you find out what I am going to do…" She indicated behind her. "…to them."

I expect she enjoyed my look, because it was a genuine spontaneous mix of horror and disbelief and panic that I couldn't hide.

Her smile thinned. "Oh yes, yes." She stood back and made a sweeping movement with her arms to show the sniffling children. And Collin, who understood precisely what was going on, began to scream and wriggle against the rope that bound him, setting off the twins who bawled a harsh cacophony of childish distress.

"You're more of an animal than your brother ever was," I said in pained disgust. "Hurt the chil—"

"Kill the children," she said, waggling a finger. "Let's be clear on that."

"And did you kill June; the woman found on the beach?"

She shrugged. "Women. Beaches. Which one? When?" She grinned into my confusion. "Lisa Gilroy, who wouldn't pay the bill or even agree to try to pay her bill?" She shrugged again. "I hit her a couple of times and she went *phewwwwww* down the cliff. But June Bailey, who nosed around the hotel and I met bin-diving one night? Odd woman. No, not personally, but you did love her too."

I fell to my knees, not believing what I was hearing.

She gave a mean laugh and I just stayed there, cowed, head suddenly ringing with a stress head-ache, mind whirling, terrified, misplacing where I was for a second, feeling outside of myself, my fear for the children so great.

"Please," I begged. "Please. Not the children. Me, okay, I'm just a stupid old woman, but not them."

"Oh, yes," she said in a satisfied voice. "Yes, this is more like it. Now put your wrinkly hands together like you're really praying, really beg-ging me." I did. "So much better in a church," she smirked. "More fitting."

I bowed my thumping head into my praying hands. 'Help me!' I yelled to anything in the uni-verse, an atavistic call to powers beyond my ken, a plea for mercy for the children.

When she'd finished enjoying the spectacle of me on my knees, the two burly men heaved me up by my elbows.

"Please," I begged again and fell down, a dead-weight sack of potatoes against their hold. Anything to give me time to think. I had escaped the major, escaped the cellar, saved myself once before. I would do it again. This time the stakes were even higher.

Chapter 16

Caving In

THE DOOR CREAKED OPEN and Stanley walked in.

My throat constricted, trying to form a combined cry of, 'Get out, you're in danger but come and rescue us!' but as he approached he said, "Sarah, this does not look like what we discussed."

So the cry that emerged from me was a strangled, "What?"

He took a step closer to the two of us. He looked at me with contempt on his face. "Scaring her? I approve. She needs taking down a peg or two."

My mouth fell open. Not my Stanley, my nice well-spoken Stanley who I had fallen in love with, he couldn't be on the bad guys' side?

"But not the children." He carried on. "To threaten—"

"Oh, I am not threatening, Stanley," she said haughtily, "I am stating. For Richard, all she loves will die: the woman, the hall, but not her son and his wife, no, she hates them so I have seen. But these little monsters she feels for so they will die, and her too." She hooked her thumb at me. "Isn't that fair, Molly?"

"No!" Stanley said angrily. "You can't do this, Sarah, I won't let you. Crush Molly, yes, that was the deal, win and break her heart, I did that, but you are not to harm the children."

"My brother," she roared, "was worth the whole town!" Her cheeks flamed with anger. "Don't block me, Stanley. You know I'll make you regret it."

"I still think it unwise," he said, jaw tight. "You will have the might of the entire police force down on our heads."

"Then what's the point of having you as my pet policeman? But no one will ever find them, thanks to your brilliant idea," she said pointedly as I knelt there listening in horror, wondering how she was going to make us disappear.

Stanley snorted. "I think—"

"You think too much. I'm in charge. Do as I say!"

"Stanley, you're a great disappointment to me," I said with my nose in the air, trying to focus the fear from the words 'only if they are found' into something else, something I could use.

"Ha!" Sarah said, her face piggish in victory, so undeserving of what I thought a pretty name. She grabbed Stanley by his coat lapels and pulled his face down to kiss him, span back to me and stuck a finger in my face. "And you will never look at my husband like that ever again!" She sniggered. "And that is a fact."

'Oh gawd,' my poor heart lamented. 'Her husband'. I didn't want to look at him ever again. Break her heart. Well done, you did that Stanley. And Sarah had been the woman in the wardrobe, of that I was now sure. Those solid thighs gave her away.

"Well, I must say, you look really good for a corpse," I managed to quip.

"I had to be dead," she sneered. "You're way too much of a goodie two shoes to even look at a married man, aren't you? And I hope you enjoyed our little show the other night," she said with twisted lips. "Oh yes, I knew you were outside listening. Did you hear what he did to me? You'll never know that kind of pleasure, will you, Molly? Old and frigid as you are."

⁓

I refused to listen to her baiting. "Darling Molly," I whispered to the floor. "Was that some kind of mean set up too?"

"Oh, the notes; they were found?" she squealed like an excited schoolgirl, turning to me to elaborate further. "My clever idea. Intimate little notes for the maid to pick up, to wonder about, to gossip about, to feed back to you, and it worked! Nice. I will have to try small town tattle-tales again."

Stanley walked off. "Wait," Sarah called after him, "you haven't told her the best bits, Stanley." He stopped with his back to us, in the stance of a man who does not want to talk.

"Come on, Stanley, the last straw—she needs it to break her completely. Get up, Molly. I want to see you fall down again when he tells you." I didn't move so I was pulled up like an old cow at a meat market. "Now, fess up, my dear husband."

His sigh was a hiss in the echoes of the old church, then he said, "I killed June."

As I slumped again, seeing Sarah's disgusting smirk, Stanley sidled into the pew to sit beside Collin and got out his notebook, beginning to write in it casually as my mind reeled and I felt I faded in and out of existence.

Sarah looked at her watch. The candles flickered all around us in the draughts. The two big ruffians shuffled their feet and rubbed their fat hands together for warmth, while the children mewled like lost kittens and the creeping cold wrapped itself round me like a shroud. Literally.

She looked at her watch again. "It's time," she snapped.

The two men dragged me bodily to the altar end of the church, beyond the pews where the children were seated, who squirmed in anticipation of rescue as I got closer, and I saw a hole in the floor exposed by the shifting of another pew. The scratch marks on the floor showed where it had been forcibly moved aside, and steps went down steeply into the yellow-red rock beneath.

"Stanley," I yelled, "do something. You can't just sit by and watch children murdered. What kind of man are you?"

His only response was to lean over and put his head in his hands. "Coward!" I shouted at him.

One of the men went in front of me with a flashlight and another pushed me down. I staggered, one hand on the damp stone wall and one holding onto my glasses, without which I would be blinder than a bat, desperately trying to keep my balance on the steps pressing me into a small space where my head grazed the roof and shadows from the torchlight showed the slant steep and long and twisting into the cliff underneath the church.

It was a long way down, the route switching back and forth as it ate into the marl bedrock, slippery in places, and I stumbled and slid until the place opened out into a cave by the light of the goon's torch. No, not a cave, there was no opening, more a hole in the ground, an inescapable hole. We were to be entombed.

Moments later the children came stumbling in after me, herded by another of Sarah's monsters, tripping over their own feet in fear so I caught them one by one as they screamed and sobbed.

"You bitch!" I screamed up the narrow, almost dark walkway as the men receded, but she was too far away, laughing no doubt, her vengeance close at hand. "And tell your bastard husband to drop dead," I roared, wondering if I could go back up the tunnel, or if I had the strength to shift the pew they would doubtless move back into position to hide us. It had to be worth a try. I heard the children getting up and felt around until I could untie them and they all hugged me.

More than a hug, really, a collection of desperate grabbing hands like I was a lifebuoy who could just float them back to the surface of their ordinary world.

Someone else was coming down the tunnel. I looked up hopefully but only saw one of the big men with a pry-bar. In no time at all he had forced a thick-hinged grid off one side of the tunnel wall and attached it to a clamp on the other side with the bar, blocking the way back up.

He vanished. All light vanished too. We were alone in a hole of dripping noises, the scents of seaweed and salt and decaying vegetation and some other noxious stench pervading the place. This had been a sea cave, once. Now it was our condemned cell.

"It's alright," I said, lying and reassuring as hard as I could, even though my fear seemed to be freezing me into inaction. "I'll get us out of here, I promise."

"Like how?" Collin muttered grumpily, his hand clasping mine in an iron grip for one so young. "It's not a video game, you know. There's no secret hidden exit and that woman took your gun so you've got no power now."

"Guns aren't power, they show weakness, an inability to fix things except by force."

He pulled away roughly. "No, it's all your fault. You should have hidden the gun in your pants or something then you could have killed that woman and we wouldn't be here now and it's all your fault!"

"Collin, really, that's not helping." My lips quivered with the guilt he was shovelling onto me.

"Dad says everything's your fault," he raged on, "Mum too. It's why they argue so much. And now we're going to die because of you!"

Chapter 17

The Trickster

I LEANED AGAINST THE WALL which dug
into my back like sharp fingers, and closed
my eyes, steadying my mind after Collin's hurt-
ful outburst, yet knowing nothing he said would
matter if we couldn't escape.

From what I had seen of the place before the
darkness covered it, the hole was about the size of
my front room, all of 20 feet square-ish, all rocky
slimy prominences.

The girls held onto me making small noises of fear. Again I said, "It'll be alright." I couldn't say anything sensible, anything true, could I?

Water sloshed somewhere close, a melodic noise that might have been quite pleasant under other circumstances. "There must have been a way in, or out, once, if it's a smuggler's cave," I said aloud. "They didn't store stuff here if it's tidal, just came in from the beach and took their contraband into the church up the passage. Likely the local vicar was in on it."

"Great," scoffed Collin. "We're stuck so we can't avoid history lessons."

I bit back a reply. Water suddenly licked at my ankles, then was gone again, the tide inching up with each wave.

"What are we going to do?" Myha suddenly screamed, panicking, stamping her feet in a staccato.

"I want Mummy!" Minnie raged.

"So do I," I muttered.

"Are we going to die?" Minnie demanded. I could hear Myha sniffling.

"No. I won't let you, sweetheart. I need you to jump on me in the morning to wake me up, don't I?"

"Good, Nana, 'cause I don't want to die. I want to see Dinosaur Valley."

"Right. Dinosaur Valley. Duly noted. I wish I could see; it would help a lot."

"Umm… Nan, I've got a lighter," Collin said in the wary voice of a child who expects to be told off.

"Great! Give it to me."

"Are you gonna yell at me?"

"Like you yelled at me just now? No. What else have you got that might be useful?"

"A penknife."

"Wonderful. I need that too."

As I felt the lighter pressed into my hand, I felt like joyfully singing, 'Boys, boys and all their toys', but when I felt the penknife my stomach did a flip flop. It wasn't a penknife by any definition. In the lighter's glow I could see it was a handle hiding a spring-loaded blade. The boys used to call them flick knives in my day. Whatever its name, it was a pretty big and dangerous knife for a little boy.

"I'm not mad, Collin, not in the circumstances, but wherever did you get this knife?"

"Errr…"

"If you stole it, you'll have to return it when we get out of here, okay?"

"No!" he said indignantly. "I don't steal things. It's a present."

"Collin, come on now, don't lie. Dad wouldn't ever let you have a knife this big."

"Not Dad, that man, that Mr Quoit who told me about the fossils, he winked at me and slipped the knife and the lighter all wrapped up in a piece of paper into my pocket when we sat in the church."

"Good grief! Okay, sorry, Collin." But why had Stanley, murderer, deceiver, husband of my enemy, done such a thing unless…

Unless he had, in his own weird way, a conscience that wouldn't let him kill children because he'd never had a family of his own.

And these strange gifts were because he knew there was a way to survive the hole.

"Nan, do you want the piece of paper too?"

By the wobbling illumination of the lighter, I read what Stanley had hastily scribbled as he sat by Collin:

"My darling Molly please forgive me I didn't know she was going to attack the children, HOLD ON, the knife can cut marl, the light can only help. Stanley."

I shut the lighter and leaned against the wall. A chuckle came from me; a demented little chuckle for the sadness of my world. Stanley had lied to me, he was married though it certainly didn't sound from the short conversation earlier that he wanted to be married to her, so I should hate him. But on the other hand he was trying to help. 'Hold on'. That had to mean he was going to rescue us. Now I loved him even more, wretched man, and hated him to point of desiring vengeance because he had killed June. This was conflicting, to say the least. What a trickster!

So, should we just wait to be rescued? Or should I be scouring every inch of the frigid hole to find some obvious means of getting us out with the knife? In any event, I had to act faster than my cold limbs wanted me to.

I hugged the children, water surging against my calves already. It was coming in fast.

"Collin," I said with urgency. "I've had an idea. Keep the girls close. I'm going to investigate."

I stood him against the wall to brace him then managed to pass the twins to him one at a time, little hands clutching feverishly at any contact, grabbing onto my clothing then having their fingers disengaged and placed where they needed to grasp on him. Then I flicked on the lighter and looked over the walls to see the algae levels; maximum high tide markers. The slimy thick green line was about level with my chest, which meant the hole was not going to fill, but I wasn't ready to cheer yet. Any water was cold at this time of the year, and since we had no way of avoiding the incursion of seawater, we would get wet, we would get cold, we might well get hypothermia—especially the skinny twins—and we could all die just as thoroughly as drowning.

"All right. You won't like this, but take off your coats and jumpers."

"Then we'll be even colder," Collin complained. "You're not dangerous, you're pathetic."

"You think I don't know that? Feel free to share your escape plan, Mr Know-it-all." I was wrestling off my coat, moving to the girls to take theirs. "Listen, if we can keep the coats dry then when the water goes back down we'll have something to bundle up in to warm ourselves, do you understand? We'll get wet, that's a given, and wet clothes will drag us down and make us even colder, so give me anything you can to keep dry, and we'll huddle up and keep sane and warm each other until the tide turns. It's quite fast, you know that."

I held the reluctantly shed clothing over my head and turned to the metal grille, forcing the coats into the gaps at the top to keep them secure and dry, and suddenly had an epiphany. Of course, 'The knife can cut marl', so I got going, scraping, sawing, working at the rock around the hinges' pins. We could get out and sit on the steps well away from the water and wait for our rescue. Job sorted.

Ping! The blade snapped off in the hinge as I slipped the knife in the wrong way.

I bit back on a swear word but Collin heard it. "What have you done wrong now, Nan?" he asked, his lack of trust in me painful but merited.

"Nothing," I lied as my mind flitted from one idea to another, dismissing my plans one by one, trying to find something else workable with the stub of a broken knife as I stepped back to the shivering children, and I turned off the lighter to hold and hug them, to pray, to beg help of the forces June had believed in so firmly, to think alone in the dark, holding Collin's hand that had never held mine so firmly before, almost feeling his demanding thoughts coming through it: Save us, Nan!

"*Nana, Nana, Nana!*" Abruptly, one of the girls started screaming. "Someone's touching me! Someone's touching my bottom!"

I instantly flicked on the lighter, only to see a blackened dead hand tapping her, its arm in the water, connected to a body drifting face down.

"Just seaweed," I said, lighter off, steering the floating corpse to the other side of the cave and

173

putting a rock on its chest to weigh it down. I think the rock sank through the rib cage but I didn't use the light to check.

Water rising, I hoisted the children onto my shoulders, my head, like monkeys grabbing and chattering, trying to keep three cold, semi-naked children out of the water's way, wondering if I had done the right thing, but what other course of action could I have taken?

My chest tightened, a feeling of nausea swept over me; an angina attack approached and I didn't have my pills. I couldn't die there, I wouldn't, I refused to, but this was something I could not control.

When was Stanley planning on rescuing us? It had to have been an hour already. Or was it—god forbid—a nasty joke? Were Stanley and his not-so-lovely wife laughing at the idea of us sitting in the cold water, waiting... numbly waiting for a rescue that was never really going to come?

I tried to relax, but the cold was attacking my insides like a frigid cancer, constricting my blood flow, starving my heart...

∽

"Nan! Nan! Naaan!" a panicked Collin screamed distantly.

With a snap, I regained consciousness as water enveloped me. No hands were on me as I stood and spluttered sea water and yelled, "Children!" fumbling for the lighter I had tucked into my bra for safety.

Collin was clambering up the grille, holding on for dear life. Minnie was on his back like a baby lemur, arms around his middle; blue arms, shaking arms, a child so cold she wouldn't be able to hold on much longer.

"You fell," Collin said, his words slurred, accusing.

"Myha?" I said, casting around in the water and finding her floating face down. Guilt and grief assailed me as I grabbed up the dead fish of a child.

The terror that had enveloped me in the major's well of corrupted water filled me even more now, a terror not for me but for the children, and all I could hear in my head was Vana screaming and Gavin's condemning voice saying, 'Mother, how could you let this happen?'

Chapter 18

Hold On

I HELD MYHA TO MY CHEST, no heartbeat in her, no breath, no place to put her down so I had to try CPR with her cradled in my arms, awkward, frightened beyond my wits, not knowing the proper procedure, never having done it on an adult, vowing to do a Paediatric First Aid course, promising those empty promises, the bargains with a god I didn't believe in. Let her live and I will never drink again, I will give more

money to charity, I will help build a new church…
Holding her awkwardly with one arm, I pressed
down on her chest with my hand, over and over
for what felt like long frigid minutes, then rubbing her, trying to get her to breathe like a new-
born puppy that looks dead, stimulating it into
action. My heart staggered again as she mewled
then threw up water.

"Myha!" I cradled her close, waded to the others and we all held each other, crying with fear
and relief. Water now up to my chest, death had
been beaten for the moment, but how many more
moments did we have to survive?

✎

The water had gone down a fraction. I felt it
leaving, like a sucking on my clothes, like being
licked by a very large dog.

As the water receded, I encouraged the freezing children to strip and put their dry clothes on
and we all found some relief; but the coldness
was not our friend. What would happen the next
time the tide came up? How many times could
we stand the torture?

For now, the children put their coats back on, we hugged, rubbed each other's arms and legs, and we huddled in a warming clump of bodies under the tent of my coat, and tried to be brave.

"The tide won't be back for a good few hours, so…" I heaved a big sigh, "all we have to do is make a tunnel through the front, and for that we can use Mr Quoit's broken knife as a digging tool."

"Until you break it again," Collin muttered. How the child sounded like his mother.

"I'm still all ears for your escape plan," I reminded him.

He didn't answer.

"I'm keeping you alive, isn't that enough?" I asked.

"More like you're trying to kill us, fainting like that."

"Collin, I am getting old and so is my heart. It doesn't like the cold. It could give out again if I don't watch out. My medicine's in my bag, my bag's with the bad guys. I am doing my best so stop complaining, for Pete's sake."

After a second his contrite voice said, "I didn't know you were ill. You should've said. I'll rescue you."

"Umm… that's kind of you," I responded, wondering if there was a hidden meaning to those brave words, or whether it was an attempt at sarcasm. "Now, the beach, I guess, has to be in this direction. You sit here, all tucked up, and build up each other's warmth and keep an eye on Myha."

I was cold, trousers wrung out but clinging damply to my legs, with only my blouse and cardigan to actually warm me, but I hoped the exercise from trying to dig would keep me warm. So I felt my way around the rocks and bumps to the theoretical opening of the cave and set to work. Loose stones I shifted to one side. The knife saved my hands from the scouring sand and finer pieces of stone and I huffed and puffed with exertion and knew my shoulders would ache diabolically later.

But then I moved another stone and a rain of them showered down, glancing blows to my head and my back, making me squeal in a most unseemly way as I scrabbled backwards.

"Nana!" came a chorus of little screams followed by Collin's, "Are you alright? Are you hit?"

"I'm fine," I said hurriedly, "just fine." I feel cuts on my face. There will be bruises too. "Don't worry, everyone, I have this in hand."

Setting to it again, elbows chafing on the wet sand, the small stones under my chest felt like boulders.

I laboured a while, the children silent under their warm pile, but I was the one suffering now. The exertion that should have warmed me froze me instead. Although I could feel the gap getting wider, deeper into the pile, I worked slowly because I knew that any second it could lose stability and come crashing down again.

Then, a wind, sharp and familiar, sudden and unexpected despite being desired, gusted into our would-be tomb and swept around the scent of salt water and the stench of the body in the corner and I felt physically sick.

Swallowing hard, I looked towards the hole I had made to the outside, darkness out there as the hours had sped on. But it was nothing helpful, unusable, a space a small troll might have navigated, but not me. I had to go extra carefully now, stone by stone—my fingers frozen, fumbling, body weakening…

"Not long now, sweethearts," I murmured. "I've made a small hole, just got to make it bigger and we can get out of this mess, okay?"

"Nan, Myha's breathing funny," Collin said.

She was panting. I rubbed her arms and legs and held her to my chest, the temperature inside the coat tent barely staving off the eternal chill. Minnie held my side and we rested there, a moment out from trying to escape, a moment needed to get my strength back as much as Myha's.

We all jumped in fright as a great groaning clatter of rocks on rock sounded, and I realised my tiny tunnel had succumbed to the weight above it. Back to square one. I could have cried, my despair was so total.

So, in the end, I got you after all. The major's mocking voice seemed to echo off the walls.

"Go away," I said aloud.

"Who, Nana?" Minnie asked.

"No one," I said.

"So where's Collin?"

I was up with the lighter on in an instant of heart-stopping, blood draining realisation. He had gone. He had tried to go through the hole and it had fallen on him! Or had it fallen when he'd got out? I didn't know anything anymore.

Near exhausted, I huddled with the girls, all of us sobbing. I knew I had to move, but I couldn't. My energy had gone out with the tide, out with Collin's possible demise. I was empty. Though this particular tide hadn't killed us, the next might, or the next. Something would get us one way or the other.

Minnie's head moved sharply. "Someone's shouting."

Yes, they were. I crawled to the wall and yelled as loudly as I could then flopped to the ground, thinking of outside, in the real world, the warmer world, the world where I would be cursed and hated by my child, but at least I had the girls; they were safe. Was that enough? No, never enough for Vana; my thoughts tumbled over each other. I was afraid of being rescued. I didn't want to be found lacking a child, I didn't want the rescuers to find his body, I remember that so keenly in those last seconds as the wall of debris was defeated, and all I could think was of my guilt in losing one, not saving two.

❧

They say that it is when the battle is finally over that you collapse. I know I did. I vaguely remember the man, the hard-hatted rescuer who broke through first and said, "Thank god; do you know how hard it's been to trace you?" but I don't remember how we got to the hospital. I only know I woke and I was warm, some kind of hot air puffer thing on me, a monitor attached to my finger. I reached for the red buzzer and a nurse appeared. "The children?" I whispered.

I saw her face drop as the monitor declared my heart's stuttering rhythm.

"The little girls are going to be fine, Mrs Smith, but the boy is in intensive care."

"What?"

The monitor beeped madly. The nurse eyed it cautiously as she went on, "I understand he was caught in a rockfall? He sustained head injuries. Some brain swelling. He hasn't woken up yet."

"He's in a coma?"

"Yes, and he'll be kept that way for a while, best way to heal, you see." She placed an encouraging hand on my arm. "Now don't you worry, there's nothing you can do and he's in the best place."

"Take him to Bournemouth."

"You don't trust our nursing experience? It wouldn't do him any favours to be moved at this point."

"Is she awake?" came a yell, and the Vana-missile was incoming, right on target.

I think if Gavin had not been with her she would have beaten at me with her sharp little fists. As it was, the nurse had to call for orderlies to remove her for upsetting me, for sending the monitor into a crazed representation of the storm inside me, where my head rang with her vileness. And the most awful thing was I knew I deserved it all.

❧

The police had come to the flat and quizzed me as to what was going on when the girls and I were released from hospital two days later, so I'd told them to talk to Sergeant Williams who would have all the details and to come back if they still needed more.

Need I mention that Gavin and Vana were still mad at me? Very, very mad at me. The children had been put at risk—no, almost killed—by their grandmother's shenanigans, an involvement Gavin had specifically told me to avoid. And, when Minnie decided to blurt out about the gun and the knife, Gavin didn't even wait until the sentence was over before assuming it was my knife and my gun that I had been wielding.

Even worse, both girls had heard me telling the voice of the major to go away, and they had turned it, in their stressed minds, into an instruction for Collin to go away, thereby causing him to try to wriggle out. I was pretty sure the voice had come after the collapse of the tunnel, but I was getting battered on all sides and arguing made me question myself. In truth, I think he had finally done something noble: he had heard me say I was ill. He heard me say there was a hole, and he had tried to rescue us.

Then came the bombshell. Marching orders for Molly. There I was thinking I had done a good job in keeping the children alive, and there were the parents disregarding the fact they were still alive… even Collin was alive, expected to make a full recovery. Fear made them angry, and the thing they feared was me.

Vana wanted me out. She'd had enough of living in fear. Gavin very regretfully sided with her. Part of me could see her point of view. It seemed pointless to argue. The crazy Sarah and her husband were still out there somewhere. Chances were, the moment she heard I'd escaped the hole and arrived home she'd come and burn down the flat, and Misty-cat, and the twins.

So I simply nodded at Gavin and Vana, looked at the twins who avoided my gaze, and went into the flat to pack. Where could I go? Somewhere interesting. The biggest problem was, I didn't have a passport so couldn't go abroad. Unlike Gavin, I had chosen to vanish completely. With no driving licence, no pension and no passport, Molly Smith was a no one.

Still, I had never gone to the Lake District, or seen Ben Nevis, or Loch Ness. That sounded interesting, and there were always bus tours to investigate.

I should have known it wouldn't go to plan. Even packing my bags turned out to be something that I soon regretted.

Chapter 19

Enough Is Enough

W HILE PACKING MY BAGS, I took out the bottom drawer of the dresser as I saw clothing slip down the gap at the back, and right at the bottom of the drawers, tucked under the edge, I found the little notebook Gavin had been looking for right at the beginning of this story.

It was small and black with an integral pencil, just like Stanley's, just like the average police notebook, and when I opened it and flicked through the pages I was struck dumb and then became very angry—incandescent with the pain of deceit and the things people put on me when it was not my fault at all.

The tiny book contained accounts of people of interest. That's what it said on the first page. There were many names and a few lines of description for each of them. One of them was Sarah Henders.

Another was Stanley Henders, tall with grey hair and grey eyes.

There were a lot of names and descriptions in that book. It appeared that Gavin had been working with the police. It would have helped matters if he'd come clean about his involvement, or maybe he'd forgotten who was in the book, and of course I had kept Stanley out of his way for fear of comment, but the last date was only the year previously. Nevertheless, I was still angry.

I was so angry that something popped in me, a mental break of outrage and despair and unfairness.

I stormed out of my flat and found Gavin in his office. He looked up as I marched in, a frown forming; and a guilty-pinched expression spreading over his face as I slammed the notebook down with as much noise as a tiny notebook can make.

"Explain this," I demanded. "You've known about these horrors for a long time. Don't you think it would have been a good idea to warn me of them?"

He waved his arms apologetically. "I couldn't, Mum. It's all supposed to be secret stuff, you know?"

"Secret?" I hollered. "From me? You have risked the children, not me. By not telling me what you knew about this organisation working in Little Kerton, you effectively precipitated all of our trouble. Even the death of June! If I'd known what was in that book, I would have never even… anything. Anything. Your silence caused it all."

"What you moaning about now, Granny?" Vana's tired voice said from the doorway where she leaned against the jamb, a study in not-caringness. "He does his job. I do mine. You watch kids. That's the deal. Not our fault you're useless at watching kids."

I rounded on her. "Did you know there's a group of thugs working in Kerton?"

I knew the answer from the fact that she glanced at Gavin and he shrugged.

"You both knew? So how could I be expected to keep the children safe against an invisible enemy! All you do is make me feel more and more guilty over something I had no control over because you two idiots thought granny was too thick to understand or keep a bloody secret."

"Yes," said Vana.

"No!" Gavin said shooting up to face her. "Stop this blaming. Now. Get back to the girls, Vana. I'll deal with this."

But a huge tidal wave of what's-the-point-of-anything was sweeping over me. I felt it drowning me, killing me more thoroughly than the cave.

I fled back to the flat, ignoring Gavin's call after me. I'd had enough. I couldn't rectify anything. Gavin and Vana hadn't been honest. If I couldn't expect it of Gavin, just who could I expect it from?

I threw a few things into a bag then threw the bag into a corner and sobbed on the bed. I felt unworthy to be even liked in any fashion. Angry son, wary grandchildren, fierce daughter-in-law; what was I to do?

Just an old woman—yes, an *old* woman—who has tried and failed to find her place in the world.

I left a short note saying I'd decided to leave them in peace and move on, then I took all the remaining medication with almost a whole bottle of wine. I looked for Misty to apologize to her. Yes, apologize to a cat. She might miss me, she might not, but she would be fine with the family. The children were very fond of her; she was tolerant of them, never peed in corners or ate the plants or scratched anything. Yes, she'd be fine.

Then I just left everything, walking off down the road without a coat or a handbag, away from my cosy little flat and the new life I had in truth begun to doubt within a month of moving in, and certainly after chaos had yet again descended on me.

Coming to the main crossroads, I took one last look back, and then walked resolutely through town, along the roads in the semi-darkness and down the path to the beach in the cold, letting the discomfort wash over and into me. I'm not brave enough to wade into the sea or jump off cliffs, so I hoped I could just sit on the beach and fade out from the drugs I could feel fizzing and fading my brain, and exposure would take me. No one would miss Molly who was cursed. Molly who got people killed. I hoped June might come visit me at the end, take my hand and lead me off, saying something sarcastic like, "There; I told you there was an afterlife. Now, come and meet some new friends."

More likely, the major would come and sit gloating, waiting for me to slip-slide away so he could drag me to hell. If I'd been killed by the major, so many nice people would still be alive.

I perched upon some cold, smooth rocks. Past crying. Past everything. I had fallen in love and found it all a trick, though the man had at least had the decency to call the coastguard to rescue us, even if it had taken so long we'd almost died anyway, and Collin could still die, realistically, and I wondered how that rescue would go down with Sarah if she ever found out. She'd gloat when she saw my demise on the news. Maybe have a party. Finish off the nude painting to celebrate…

The sea hissed on the sand suck suck hiss, the clouded sky hung dark and stormy, and farther down the beach I saw pin-point lights dancing, torchlight, night time beachcombers, and then I heard a voice from above.

"Oi, Ms T, wotcha doing down there?"

"Oh, Hugo," I breathed to the imagined voice. "I didn't think you'd come for me. But I suppose I did love you in my grandmotherly way. I am so sorry about what happened to you."

The clouds twisted, stars shone through, Hugo's face loomed in the half light as he extended a phantom hand.

"Come on, let's be getting you in the warm. Not good for old ladies to be out in the cold, is it?"

"I'm alright now you're here, dear." My voice seemed to flutter. "Just sit by me. I guess it'll all be over soon. Peace; that's what I want."

"Oi, Georgie," his voice called, rattling my ears. "Come give us a hand. You're right, it's Ms T, but she's acting right weird."

A dark figure appeared outlined against the sky, a spectral man, Hugo on the good side and Georgie on...

No. Wait.

George was Hugo's roommate. He'd looked after Misty during that fracas in Hartpury. He wouldn't be on the bad side, and why was he dead too?

"No," I sobbed, tears turning to ice on my cheeks. "Not another victim of the curse."

Somebody took my head gently and a blurred bearded face peered into my spectacles. "Come on, what you taken?"

"I wanted to go."

"Go where?"

"Heaven," I murmured, and smoothly slid into oblivion.

Chapter 20

The Nice Psychiatrist

I WOKE ON A CLOUD. A nice soft fuzzy white cloud that smelled a bit like disinfectant. I kept still, listening to an alarm going beep beep beep nearby, vaguely wondering where I was and, if this was heaven, where were the harps and angels, Hugo and George and June?

A second later my brain kick-started into cognizance and I realised what I heard was a heart monitor, the world only fuzzy from lack of spectacles.

'Hospital; again,' I thought as I lay in the crisp white-sheeted bed with rose spattered curtains around my cubicle. Had I dreamed of Hugo and George or had I been so close to passing over that they'd been able to visit from the other side? June would have been ecstatic to have heard about that. The blurry memories made me cry again. I rubbed the tears away with the back of my hand and felt the cannula in my arm shift a little, and I cried more, feeling useless and done in.

A dark-haired nurse side-twisted through the curtains, a cheery smile gracing her pretty face, but it dropped when she saw my wet cheeks. She offered me water and a tissue then hesitantly smiled again when I asked for chocolate cake. She went off and came back with a lidded cup of water. Sitting half propped up, squinting at the IV line running into my left arm (the bag said sodium chloride), I drank the water through a straw as she checked on the machine beside me, noting details on the chart she unhooked from the end of the bed rail.

"Where am I?" I asked.

"Royal Bournemouth," she said. "Do you know why?"

"Not the faintest," I lied. If I admitted to an attempt at suicide, no matter how feeble, they'd cart me along to the Pysch ward.

"Do you know your name? Why you were crying just now?"

"Umm…" I was wary, nervous. The other thing to consider was, who else might be knocking around that might want a piece of me? Where was the awful Sarah hiding? Where had Stanley vanished to? What would Gavin and Vana think of me now? Did Gavin have the power to shove me into an old folks' home on the basis of mental infirmity?

"My memory is very blurry," I lied. The nurse removed the empty water cup, gave me a mechanical cheerful smile and left, opening the curtains to a blurry view of other beds, other faces, all old ladies. "I am in the wrong ward," I said aloud. "I am not old."

Somebody with a sense of humour laughed.

I managed to wriggle around to get my chart, and squinted at the words: Jane Doe. Of course, I'd had no bag, no ID.

"Look in the locker," crackled a very old voice from the bed next door, where a grinning white haired blob could be made out. "Glasses," the blob said. "I know that look. You're missing your glasses."

I thanked her and retrieved my spectacles from the locker.

"I'm Joan," the perky owner of the old voice said, and held out a hand to me.

"Jane," I responded without hesitation, and took the offered dry and wrinkly hand for a bare second.

The nurse reappeared. "Making friends?" she said. "That's good. Now, umm…"

"Her name's Jane," Joan said, brightly helpful.

"Okay, Jane, there's a consultant here to see you. Would you prefer to be in the day room for your assessment; out of the public eye? We've got no private rooms at the mo. I'll get a wheelchair for you." She went off before I'd even replied.

Me, in a wheelchair? How undignified.

But there I was, in the wheelchair, hospital dressing gown over the other gown that has only ties at the back so everyone can see your bum if you're not careful, and the tall stand thing with wheels that runs along beside you with a saline drip feeding into your arm. I felt as presentable as a dead mouse.

The white coated man waiting in the dayroom was very nice and young and polite, and introduced himself as Doctor Kellow, the consultant psychiatrist.

Uh oh, be careful, Molly.

He plonked his lanky frame down in a padded chair and took up his clipboard and a pen from his jacket.

Reading from the clipboard, and calling me Jane, he told me in a solemn, serious voice that he was there in response to another doctor's request due to concerns over my toxicology report. It had showed alcohol and benzodiazepine. He said how I'd been delivered into A&E at 23:32 hours by evening beachcombers after being found unresponsive. My stomach had been pumped, which likely saved my life.

"Was it a sincere attempt to take your life?" he asked over the board, pen poised to write my response. "Or were you hoping to make a point to someone? A cry for help, maybe?"

It had been concluded from the state of my face that I might well have been the victim of some abuse. So, how much did I actually remember? Did I want the police called? Would I like to discuss my feelings?

When I didn't immediately reply he leaned forwards, his expression pleasant and caring. "You're in a safe place, Jane. My role is the assessment and management of all patients for whom significant risk is identified, including patients who are at risk of harming themselves, harming others, or are vulnerable to neglect."

All I could think was, this meant no one had connected me to the same woman who'd escaped a hell-hole and been questioned by police in Kerton cottage hospital the day before. Was it really only the day before? I was a bit confused.

I still didn't know if I should say my real name. Hadn't Gavin missed me yet? The clock high on the pale green wall said 10:02AM. If this was Sunday, it could be everyone at Ardeal House thought

I was sulking in my room so they weren't bothering with me. Or they could think I'd upped and left already and didn't care. When they noticed the note, though, they'd be sure to contact the police (wouldn't they?) so for now I played the fuzzy memory card. I didn't want to go into all the explanations, it was too much for me, and without even having to fake them I collapsed into tears again.

Ignoring my distress, Dr Kellow scribbled on his clipboard, then said quietly, "Jane, I'd like to have you transferred to my clinic. It's only in the new annexe. I'll take you down to the concourse myself if you like; call a porter to take you the rest of the way?"

"Like this?" I spluttered, drying my face on the gown.

"It's all hospital grounds; no one will bat an eyelid."

"Not on your Nelly," I blurted. "Unless I'm unconscious I'm going out with clothes on. Nurse!" I hollered, and a different one came to my call. "Please take out this drip, I'm off with Dr Kellow and I don't want it banging into anything as it hurts anyway, and do you happen to have any clothes I could have? Are mine around? I'm not gallivanting down the road in this inelegant ensemble."

She gave Kellow a look. He nodded and she removed the drip, saying, "I'm sorry, but there's nothing else to wear. Maybe you can call a relative to bring something in later."

"Fat chance," I muttered.

She twisted the chair's foot supports around from the sides and placed my feet in them firmly. "There, all ready for the Grand Prix now. I'll see to your paperwork" She pulled a quick smile at me, positively beamed at Dr Kellow, then slipped out.

I was breathing heavily. Some sixth sense was prickling me, though to be fair it could be simply the idea of being confined in a wheelchair that made me feel incredibly defenceless. I wondered if fear was something soldiers got used to, and old ladies simply couldn't. Yes, I said old. I did feel it then. Old and vulnerable.

The original nurse reappeared with what I took to be transfer papers. Dr Kellow signed them, then she left with an almost genuine, "Good luck, Jane."

"Actually, I really would like a blanket," I said, looking at Dr Kellow hopefully. "It looks chilly outside."

He glanced out of the window at the grey-sky day then turned back to me with a weird smile. "Don't worry, Molly. Where you're going you won't feel the cold."

Chapter 21

Hellchair Ride

D r KELLOW TOOK a hypodermic needle from a pocket and waggled it before my face before jabbing it through the gown and into my thigh.

"Just a nice little local to keep you down," he said. "So you can talk and yell all you like, but not run."

"So who are you in the miserable band of bad guys?" I asked as I felt numbness chill my leg.

I wasn't going to give him the satisfaction of trying to run and falling all undignified with my petite derriere showing.

"So you are in there, Molly Marshman," he said. "I knew you were faking. My real name is the same as my dad's. Richard Sanderson Junior at your service, you pesky murderous old bitch."

It's funny—depending on your definition of funny—how many people thought I had murdered the major when in reality he'd done it to himself while trying to kill me.

"Nurse!" I yelled.

"They'll just think you kooky, Molly."

He took the wheelchair handles and whisked me out.

"He's a fake!" I shouted to the nurses at their station, who looked at me with sympathy before looking away. "He's a fraud, I tell you. Call the police!" I yelled along the corridor, a little old lady pushed by a strapping white-coated psych-consultant. Ha! What was the likelihood of a gang boss's son becoming a psychiatrist? Diagnose your own father as a sociopath, why didn't you? That's if he was a real shrink, and from the nurses' reactions they'd certainly seen him before. But had the nurses even been real nurses? Was I even Molly?

I threw myself out of the chair, sprawling, catching myself with my arms. He got a passing porter to help get me back in the chair as I gabbled, "He's not a real shrink, you know. He's kidnapping me." But the man looked at me as if I were really mad and hurried on.

"Keep going, Molly," Junior said jauntily, his steps even as he marched along. "I am really enjoying this. Should have got it on camera for Aunty."

Little did he know I was enjoying it, too. All the shouting was kind of therapeutic. I was finding the will to fight returning.

"Stop this chair right now," I bawled at the top of my lungs to the hospital audience, "you lily-livered coward who only beats up old ladies 'cause he hasn't got a dick!"

Down to the open expanse of concourse we went, the crazy old lady in me loudly calling to anyone around that I was being abducted, kidnapped, stolen, nobbled, shanghaied… Of course, no one listened. Many ignored, some gave glances then looked away. I had expected no less. People don't want to get involved. They assume everything's being handled by someone else.

Where was I being taken? A quick death, to my mind, would have been lethal injection in the hospital, to mimic a heart attack, drawing no suspicions at my age. But being taken out and away could only mean something far worse was waiting for me. It wasn't going to be anywhere nice, of that I was certain. Somewhere I wouldn't feel the cold.

"You're a ghastly excuse for a son, you know?" I said loudly. "You never visit your mother in hospital and now you're dragging her out to kill her. What will everyone think of you now?"

That got a few puzzled looks.

I tipped out of the chair again, cussing silently as it bruised my bruises.

"Shut this or I'll fucking handcuff you to it," he growled as I was hauled up again, kicking best I could and yelling until a porter ran over to help.

"Get your hands off me," I screamed at him. "He's molesting me, everybody. This man just put his hands on my tushie."

"Kerrist," Junior swore and shoved me roughly back in the chair. "Bad day for er… challenging patients, eh?" he said to the porter and walked on.

She was waiting for us outside the main doors. All dressed up in a beige silk trouser suit and with make-up on, Sarah honestly didn't look too bad as she greeted her nephew with a pat on the cheek and a big, toothy smile.

"What, no Stanley?" I said in as sarcastic voice as I could muster. She whapped me across the back of the head. "You'll never see him again," she snapped.

Taking over the wheelchair's handles, Sarah began to push me along the path skirting the hospital wall.

"Aliens!" I screamed. Heads turned. "I'm being abducted. Help!"

Sarah laughed. "I'm actually happy to see you alive and well, Molly," she said chattily, "because now I can really have some fun with you. This time we'll try something a little more permanent; more thorough, without the complication of small children."

I wondered how much she'd cackle if I told her I'd tried to kill myself the night before. Now I knew what impending death felt like, if that was where I was destined to end the day, it was nothing to fear. Friends would be waiting for me.

A piggy snort managed to escape my nose as I inwardly laughed. She thwacked the back of my head again. I assume no one noticed or, if they did, no one came to the rescue of the crazy old lady who'd recently been shouting about aliens abducting her.

I was also thinking she ought to shut up and get on with it. In all the movies, the bad guy spends far too long telling his victim what he's going to do with them and subsequently gives them to time to escape.

Around the corner the wheelchair and I sped under her guidance, past the services' entrance, past A&E where the ambulances stood waiting for calls.

I was practising flexing my thighs, fighting for some control as the short-acting drug Junior had administered showed signs of already wearing off, when someone shouted, "Gerroff!"

The wheelchair jerked up and back and down again with a rattling jar that almost sent me flying, and Sarah was no longer pushing me, her silk-trousered legs inexplicably sprawling in the road beside me as I sat numbly in the wheelchair trying to understand what was going on and a whomp—

A shriek…

A crashing bang all behind me, and people were running and screaming around me.

Someone took the wheelchair handles, whispered, "It's all right, we gotcha," in a soft male voice, and smartly wheeled me along and, as we crossed the road at an angle to the hospital, the chair was turned so I could see why people had screamed. Sarah's body lay under the wheels of an ambulance that had crashed into a pillar of the A&E's portico.

"Clever, huh?" my male pusher said. "Runaway ambulance, handbrake left off, rolled off; no one'll suspect a thing."

"What?" I squeaked.

"Not far now."

"Who…?"

"Later, later. Just round this corner…"

I was pushed through an unofficial gap in the hedge that surrounded the car park and came face to face with the smiling expression of a sunshine yellow Micra's bonnet, looking rather like one of those friendly anthropomorphic trains in children's shows.

I reached a floppy hand to the Micra as we moved alongside it.

"Hello, nice Micra. You remind me of someone I used to know."

Then the person who jumped out of the passenger door startled me so much that, had I been standing, I would have fallen over.

"Lo, Ms T, long time no see." He beamed a friendly and delighted smile into his beard. "Let's be 'aving you on board the magical mystery tour then."

"Hugo! You're not dead?" It was feeling like an hallucination. "How can you not be dead?"

The small time crook who had helped me in Hartpury shook his head firmly. "Not the last time I looked, no. You saw me and Georgie on the beach, 'member? Come on, let's be 'aving you. Explanations later."

He and George hoisted me up and pushed and pulled me into the Micra, while I tugged my dressing gown around me and tried to hide my scraggy bum from their sight.

Chapter 22

Happy Hugs

$\mathcal{B}$y the time I was safely bundled into the back seat of the Micra, and we had driven sedately out of the car park after paying at the gate machine, my leg's power had almost returned.

"Same car?" I asked. "But it's not blue?"

"Just a re-spray to confuse people," George said easily.

"You changed the reg-plate, I hope?"

"Nah," Hugo talked over his shoulder at me. "Too much 'assle. Just keep it dirty so can't be read."

"That's an offence."

"That's my Ms T," Hugo laughed.

"I would have said it was a good idea to bring me to Bournemouth hospital not Kerton, but I guess 'they' just always know where I am."

He nodded. "Did think you'd be safer 'ere."

"Fail in all directions," George said.

"How come you escaped the major's wrath?" I asked George.

"I scarpered when Kat said Major Pissed Off had grabbed Hugs. Hugs had to track me down later."

"Kat was worth her weight in gold." I thought of the young woman who'd been practically held captive by the major. "Hope she did okay."

"Deported," Hugo said dolefully.

"That's sad. Oh, clothes?" I asked suddenly. "Or is Molly to stay mainly undressed for life?"

"We'll go get yer togs."

"And Misty," George said. His smile was all white teeth in his handsome black face. Take a few years off me, around fifty, and I would be enamoured of him.

"Misty in a car? In a Micra? The basket alone would hardly fit. Wait—Are you running off with me?"

Hugo nodded. "Yer'll be safer with us than with anyone, since half the bloody population round 'ere seem to be in the cartel's pocket."

"Hmm… yes, even the shrink that got me out of the ward, a chap calling himself Kellow, claimed he was the major's son."

Hugo frowned and shrugged. "No idea 'bout that. And, Georgie, well done on taking out Madam Sarah the bitch-cow fuckwit; nice moves, man!"

"It was an accident, honest," he said with a devilish grin. "That ambulance wasn't locked and the handbrake was dodgy, just an accident waiting to happen."

"And was her falling an accident too?" I asked.

"Of course." He rotated his shoulder and grimaced. "That was one hefty lady. Likely had trouble with her centre of gravity. Think that accident nearly put my shoulder out."

We all laughed, then George said, "Fate, Ms T, only fate, only karma seeing to it that people get what they deserve. Nice things as well as bad."

As he said those words, I caught something in the look he gave Hugo.

"What are you two doing here anyway?" I asked.

Hugo drew in a deep breath and crinkled up his beard in a smile reflected in the rear view mirror. "Been keeping half an eye on you, after hearing some stuff on the grapevine. Since George and me, we got evicted, 'cause the landlady… well, she found out that…" He hesitated.

"Found out you're criminals?"

George shot me a worried look. "Well, yes and no, but that wasn't what she was worried about."

"How many guesses do I get?" I asked.

The two men exchanged glances and I made an inspired guess. "You're a couple. Congratulations. Can I be a bridesmaid? I've never been a bridesmaid."

"You feeling alright there?" George asked me.

I smiled the biggest smile I could, thinking how this little revelation made me happy for them, after the pain of the cave and everything that had happened to me, I was going to be saved by this loving couple.

"I'm happy for you," I said. "That's all."

"So the homophobic landlady chucks us out and you want to be our bridesmaid," George chortled. "You're amazing, Ms T."

"Thank you, kind sir. I believe in the philosophy that one loves who one loves." Stanley, Stanley, how could you hurt me so much? "So come on, tell me, boys, how'd you survive? Escape the group, cabal, coven, whatever they were?"

"Drug runners," Hugo began. "The lot you an' me upset—yeah, not like me, I was just muscle and I didn't deal with dirty stuff. Needle and Jim and the other two lads did, though. Anyhoo, they work in a messy world full of fear, hurt an' pain; sure you noticed that." He glanced at me, then his eyes went down again beneath his beetling brow as if he was ashamed of the things he was telling me. And he might well have been.

"Damned if you tell and damned if you don't tell," he said and went on sadly. "All the time, constant on the edge of yer seat kind of fear, of being bumped off, of being arrested, of doing something boss man don't like, all wears on yer nerves. Not a good way to make money, to live. Sitting back and watching them destroy your life…" He shook his head. "Yer mates' lives too. Nah, I couldn't deal with it no more. I was trying to escape when I took the dosh; me retirement fund I reckoned. I wanted even more to escape when they caught you, 'cause that was all my fault."

"But the major said he'd overdosed you. The boots, sticking out of the ground?"

He sighed heavily. "He sent two blokes out to bury me—you know 'em, other two from searching yer house—but they realised I weren't dead and cause they sorta knew me they didn't want to bump me off final-like and took me to the hospital where some coppers 'appened to be for something unrelated, but taking me in was so suss the lads got nicked. They told on what the major had wanted them to do with me, so the cops buried the boots and put out that I was dead as a way to lure him in, or summit."

"Ah, I see. Would you believe, I have a picture of you on my wall?"

"How'd you manage that?" he frowned. "Mug shot?"

"I got an evidence copy from the police," I said. "It's just the boots sticking out of the mud. But I don't need it now I have the real thing."

I leaned back in the seat.

"There's just one last question now," I said quietly, almost to myself. "Where's Stanley, and is he likely to come after me? He saved us from the cave but, now Sarah's been killed—at least, I suppose she's been killed; being run over by an ambulance likely has that effect on a person—will he want to get back at me for that?"

Chapter 23

Catching The Bus

THE MICRA DREW UP outside Ardeal House. Neither of the family cars were there, so no one was in. I unlocked the door with the hidden spare key and found my stomach sinking as I walked in.

No one had even bothered to look in my room. My goodbye note was still anchored to the bedside table by my phone. I could have died in my sleep for all they knew; been on the way to becoming a mouldering corpse like the one in the cave.

I gathered some clothes and slung them into my smallest suitcase, tore up the old note and wrote another. I simply said I had gone to stay with friends. No lie there.

I considered keeping the phone but it was full of memories of Stanley.

And just where is he?

No, don't wonder, leave that subject well alone and go off on another adventure. Remember: friendships trump love. Okay?

Misty made her presence known. I gathered her soft fluffiness into my arms and knew I could not take her with me, no matter how much George might think it a good idea, so I put her outside and locked the cat-flap so the family would have to let her in later. Then they'd look for me.

I went back out to the Micra dressed and ready.

"Where's Misty?" George asked with a look of intense disappointment.

"I'm sorry, but I honestly can't see her travelling with us. A dog might, but not a cat."

He pouted. "I am… bereft."

I slung my belongings into the boot, climbed into the back seat and said, "Wagons ho!"

"Wagons wot?" Hugo said.

I am so going to enjoy educating these lads.

"Wagons ho was what the wagon train leaders would yell to get the settlers' wagons moving when the west was first being colonised."

"So…" He started the engine. "Micra ho!"

We stopped at the cliff-top cafe because I was very hungry, and I'm ashamed to say I ate like a horse (or a man). In between bites I filled the boys in with what had happened to me, though I couldn't help but keep looking around, nervous, suspecting everyone who came in of intending ill towards me. I had attempted to disguise myself with a headscarf and really red lipstick. I'd have done the dark glasses bit too, but I didn't have any.

I borrowed a phone to call the hospital, to check on Collin, but no one would talk to me other than to say he was still alive, but that was some comfort. George patted my back. He was into patting. "Don't fret so, Ms T. Lad'll be fine. My mum, she got kicked by a horse a few years back. Right in the head. Out for a week, she was, fine as rain after."

"That's reassuring. Thanks. Now, shouldn't we be getting out of town?"

"Slow and steady-like," George cautioned. "Rushing around is suss." He let his hand stay on my back like calming a cat.

Filled with foreboding like an evil doughnut, fear crept into my system and made me feel sick, though it could have just been the food I'd eaten too fast.

"I need to be somewhere nicer," I complained, "not full of bad memories. Let's go now. Please?"

'Where's all your fire gone, Molly?' I asked myself. 'It wasn't that long ago you were promising yourself you'd never be scared of anything ever again.' And I suddenly realised I wasn't scared for me, but for these two lads who had seen fit to rescue me just because they liked me. Family isn't just blood; it's people who grow on you.

"Okay," Hugo said. "Got a little job to do. You look after Ms T, Georgie, and I'll be back in two shakes of a lamb's tail."

"Pick up my special backpack while you're at it, right?" George asked. "You know, just in case?"

"You're not gonna need that," Hugo scoffed as he stood up. "Bet you fifty you don't need it."

"You're on," George winked at him.

Hugo stood and looked down at me with a curious expression I couldn't read. "See ya later," he said, and off he went.

"What is he up to?" I asked George quietly. "Is it something illegal? It's something illegal, isn't it, the way he looked at me, like he wanted to apologise for doing it before he did it?"

George huffed a laugh. "I dunno. Might be he just wants to get a crate of beer for the trip. I love him, but he baffles me too sometimes. You want pudding? I fancy pudding. They got apple pie?" He stared up at the menu board.

A shiver ran through me as I remembered the last time I had been in the cafe, scared of being followed, wanting the security of Stanley beside me, all a lie. I doubted there ever had been any-one following me. The danger had been beside me all the time. I was a fool. Maybe I was also a fool for trusting the lads, but I would never know until afterwards and I just felt that I was… almost one of the gang, somehow.

I ordered a pot of coffee and stared at the brown stuff circling in my cup more than I spoke to George. He made up for it by talking, on and on, about the adventures the two of them had been on together in the past year, how Hugo had actually, really, fancied Katarina and was dis-traught when she'd been 'thrown back over the sea', as he put it.

"Hang on," I interrupted. "I'm confused now. If he's with you, how can he have fancied Kat?"

He shrugged. "You can love more than one person, right? He'd have moved her in with us, given half a chance."

I decided I was stepping out of the bounds of my knowledge of modern love, so let the matter drop.

Then George went on about how he'd wanted to get a kitten, in the hope it'd cheer Hugo after

Kat had gone, and I saw he was a caring young man, no matter what his past crimes might have been.

About an hour and a half later, after drinking too much coffee to perk myself up, and too much apple pie with cream to make myself full-belly happy, Hugo returned with a backpack that he handed to George, and a new, startling appearance. Despite his beard and overall facial hairiness, the bruising on his face was obvious. I looked at him in alarm as he eased himself into the seat opposite me, squeezing George over.

"And what in heaven's name have you been up to now?" I asked.

He gave a pained laugh and raised a finger to his battle-wounds. "Not sure, but the other geezer's unconscious, so reckon I won."

"Why and what the hell, Hugo?" Great start to the relationship.

I turned to George. "Does he do this often?"

"Lady's asking, Hugs."

Hugo lowered his head and said quietly, "All in the name of honour, Ms T. That doc, the shrink what gave you grief. I nipped to the 'ospital, found 'im, gave 'im a few love pats and chucked 'im in a nice big waste bin."

"Oh Hugo," I cried, clapping my hands together. "I do love you!"

"Yeah," he said, a light coming into his eyes as he saw my approval. "It was boof!" He shot out his arm in a punch. "Then bash! That's for Molly, you rotter, and bosh!" He play-punched George. "That's for Molly, too, you stinking bastard."

"Excuse me," said an annoyed, cautioning voice from behind the counter, "but could you gents keep your voices down. You're disturbing the other customers."

"Nipping to the loo," George grinned, and left with the backpack. I would find out eventually what was in it; 'just in case'.

Chapter 24

True Love

W E LEFT THE CAFE, and drove to the town's bus rank, where a big green out-of-service bus waited. I watched in confused fascination as Hugo began to attach the Micra to a tow bar on the rear of the bus.

"Isn't that rather a giveaway, if anyone's looking for you?" I asked.

"Nah, I'll just get it sprayed another colour later," Hugo said. "Wotcha think? Pink next time, for a lady, huh?" He laughed, and as I stood there with my mouth open to lecture him on the foolishness of thinking the BBGs wouldn't be able to track him 'somehow' through his precious little Micra, George prodded me and mouthed, 'Don't bother,' then unlocked the bus door and we boarded.

"A bus house!" I exclaimed as the internal conversion was revealed. "It's beautiful."

"Yeah," Hugo grinned and winced as the action caught his bruise. "Amazing what you can get off internet auctions, innit?"

I laughed. "Still, it must've cost a pretty penny." I admired the kitchen section at the front, almost as nice as my own— As my own had been, I revised with a jolt. Just as I was wondering how much a single-decker bus and its conversion ran to, George said softly, as if the world was listening in. "He's still had some of the major's diamonds, you know? Didn't all fit in that hidey hole."

"Well, I think this is amazing. Where are the beds?" I asked. "I'm done in. Just need a power nap."

"Past the bathroom; that slidey door." Hugo pointed to the back of the bus, so I walked up the middle with my bag and dropped it on a settee.

Stanley emerged from the sliding door like the xenomorph appearing in 'Alien'. It had about the same effect on me. I staggered and reached to a wall cupboard for support.

I glanced back where Hugo and George were as frozen as I was, because Stanley held my pistol loosely in one hand.

I took a deep breath and jumped in. "Oh, thank you, Stanley, that's mine." I extended a hopeful hand. "Can I have it back, please?"

"Get off the bus, Molly," he said coldly, his eyes on the boys more than me.

"How'd you get on? The door was locked."

He gave me a deprecating look. "Did you imagine a simple door lock could defeat me? Come on, Molly, get off this effrontery to British style. We have places to go, things to see."

"What?"

"Sarah's dead; a traffic accident. We're free. Where shall we go?"

"Fucking hell," George whispered. "He wants to run off with you, Ms T."

"What's the idiot saying?" Stanley demanded. The pistol raised its ugly snout.

"Listen," I said in a gently placating voice, "I don't want to run off with you, because I have decided to run off with my friends here."

"These simpletons?" he asked, astonished. "These raging homosexuals?" His mouth curled in disgust around the word. "Huggy showed some promise at first, but once he set up with that black thing." He indicated George. "He was lost to our cause."

"Stop insulting them," I said, hard put not to rage at this pompous and bigoted man I'd thought I'd loved. "You haven't been honest, Stanley, and I can't be with yet another dishonest man, and put that wretched pistol down. You're not going to shoot anybody. That would be rude."

His face crumpled. I actually thought he was going to cry. "I love you, Molly," he said. "Sincerely and utterly, it is no lie. Your kindness, your humour, your open humanity; so much more than

Sarah ever had. You treat me as an equal, not a slave. Let us be each other's company into aging. We deserve each other."

"There's another great big problem, Stanley. A really enormous problem. You killed June. I can't forgive that."

"Sarah made me do it."

"Made you?" I was incensed at the passing of blame. "Like, she stood there with a gun on you and said 'Push her off or you die'?"

"Freddy was supposed to—"

"The burglar, right, and why'd he go over the cliff too? Was there an orderly British queue or something?"

He glared at me. "You do not know how things are."

"If the major's shenanigans were anything to go by, then by golly yes, I do."

"Then you will understand that Freddy did not do what he was told. He refused to kill June, so I had to remove both of them, but I did not enjoy it."

My hand had covered my mouth in horror. "Wha... what the actual hell, Stanley! You are stood there asking me to run off with a murderer. How do you think I could ever do that?"

"Because the group will never stop looking for you, and you can be safe with me, I assure you. I would be no worse than your first husband. I knew Oswald well, and wondered at the undeserving way he spoke of you."

"No, no, my head is spinning," I complained, fitting all the pieces together like a warped jigsaw puzzle. "Was there ever a man following me?"

"Of course not, the ambition of that exercise was to bond you to me."

With a crazy laugh I declared, "An unfortunate success."

I looked back at the lads, who stood stock still with blankly despairing faces.

"I must be crazy," I said, beginning the show I had come up with in a millisecond, "but if you'll keep me safe, okay. You have intelligence, style, and I did fall for you, so you win. Now give me the gun, just to be on the safe side, and I'll come with you. See there? I have a little bag packed already. It'll do."

Stanley gave a suspicious growl.

"You're going with him?" George squawked. "I wouldn't trust him as far as I could throw him."

I said gently, "I'm a big girl, George." Then I whispered, "I think he'll shoot you both to get me."

"Stop whispering," Stanley ordered.

"So give me the gun," I repeated. "I'm coming with you; once I get over all the horrid things you've done, we can have wonderful days on the beach together, talk about rocks and trains and anything we like, right?" I held out my hand to receive the gun and his eyes flickered over all of us.

"You're giving me the chance of a new life, Molly," he said. "I cannot express my gratitude adequately. But one of the rules of my world is, no loose ends."

He shot George.

I screamed and leapt in front of Hugo, shielding him, saying tightly, "Keep still. He won't shoot me."

I hadn't managed to save Collin, but I'd be damned if I didn't protect Hugo.

"Georgie…" Hugo whimpered.

"Stay. You can't do anything for him."

"Molly," Stanley ordered. "Step away. If you truly desire a life with me, accept the bearded oaf's life is forfeit."

"No!" I snapped over my shoulder. I span round, my arms out wide, still trying to shield Hugo. "If you truly desire a life with me, he lives. Get it?"

"Whatever do you see in him?"

'All of the things I don't see in you', I thought, but I said, "Go on, Hugo, off the bus with you, and I will follow in two ticks."

Hugo and I retreated to the front of the bus, Stanley walking slowly towards us, the pistol still raised.

"Get off, Hugo!" I whispered. "He'll be out in a min. I saw a big bin alongside the toilet block." He got my meaning and reached for the door button as I tried to distract Stanley with, "Did you know, Collin's in the ICU, in a coma? The rescue came too late for him."

Hugo jumped out.

"I did my best," Stanley said defensively, the pistol loose at his side again. "It's the fault of the rescue services. I gave them as much information as I could and assumed they'd have some kind of ground penetrating radar, infra red or the like."

"Maybe he'll wake if you tell him fossil stories."

"I might make a terrible grandfather, but I shall be a most excellent husband, I guarantee." To my surprise and relief, he turned the pistol round and gave it to me, handle first. "A peace offering," he said.

As I accepted it, I looked at the fallen, beautiful George. I thought of Hugo out there waiting to deal with Stanley to avenge him. I thought of June, my lovely friend, beaten and thrown over a cliff; Lisa Gilroy, who had just wanted motherhood and paid the price with her life; bereaved husbands, terrified soaking children, injured children who Stanley-the-deceiver thought were less than snakes...

So I shot Stanley Quoit because he deserved it, point blank, twice to make sure, my ears deafened by the first shot hardly hearing the second, looked at the slumped, empty thing he had become with tears finally welling in my eyes, then got off the bus to find Hugo.

Although my shaking knees were threatening to drop me, I felt no shame. I did feel loss, though. Now he was gone, the dream from weeks before finally made sense… the sinking numbing knowledge of loss showing he is with me no more… Love, hate, all confused into a little ball of life at its worst.

A man walking past stopped and looked at me in concern. "You all right, missus?" he asked.

I smiled weakly and he walked on. No one was bothered with our drama, I realised. Outside the tragedy unfolding within the bus, no one had even registered the shots. No one else cared about our little painful world.

"Bloody hell, that smarts," said a pained voice on the bus, and I looked up in amazement to see George, alive, upright, one hand to his chest.

"Okay," Hugo said, stepping up to his partner, "I bet that bloody 'urt. You'll be 'aving a bruise the size of a dinner plate under there. I were wrong. You did need it."

"Need what?" I gasped. "What's going on?"

George opened his shirt with a pained flourish, grinning from ear to ear, showing a black vest of a kind I had only ever seen before on TV. "Bullet proof vest, Ms T. Like I said: Just in case. And now Hugs owes me fifty."

Chapter 25

Homeward Bound

S TANLEY FLEW OVER THE CLIFF in the rain-
storm that blew in later that night. He
hadn't earned his wings; it was only Hugo and
George going, "One, two, three and away you
go!" launching him into the dark night. We didn't
think he'd earned any better way to be found than
that of his victims.

Death was probably the best place for a confused man like him. I hoped Sarah gave him a

hard a time in hell for 'loving' me, if he'd even understood what love was.

"Right," said George, all business like as we reboarded the bus. "First stop, somewhere to chuck the bloody carpet then, tomorrow, somewhere to buy new carpet."

I looked out of the window as the bus rumbled up Main Street and turned towards the by-pass, headlights illuminating the town, making it look far more interesting than it really was, thinking, 'Goodbye, Kerton, no thanks for all the memories,' then I yelled, "Stop!"

I jerked forward as the brakes jammed on.

"What's going on?" Hugo yelled from the driver's seat. "Forget yer toothbrush?"

"No," I said, half way to the door. "We left someone behind." I pressed the open button and called Misty, who I had seen running up the road. She galloped up to the steps, hesitated, then gingerly clambered on board.

I scooped her up. She purred and rubbed into my cheek. George practically grabbed her from me, but I said nothing.

"Okay…" Hugo said resignedly. "Any more passengers before I starts off again? No chickens or frogs or butterflies?"

I shook my head. "I think I have everything I want now, everything that makes my life, my life, though we'd better find an open pet-store for supplies for madam here."

"Supermarket," George said. "24 hour thingy, outskirts of Lyndhurst. Maybe 20 mins?"

"Lyndhurst? Where are we off to, then?"

"Surrey. Got some business in Bracknell."

We set off again, and I tried to imprison Stanley in the farthest reaches of my mind, hoping I'd forget him, like when I put the butter in the freezer by accident, or fed Misty Collin's cereal and him the dry cat food. But I know that deep down I won't forget the good feelings he gave me before I found out who he was. So I'm seventy something, does that mean I'm not allowed to love? At my age and after my life experiences, I think I need it, deserve it, am owed it by fate.

But for the moment I was home. It was a home aboard a converted bus with two petty criminals and my beloved cat, but June had been right. Friends are the best.

And friends that support you even when they know you're a murderer are even better. If you'd told me a few years ago that I would have had the guts to kill Stanley, I would have laughed and run away from you.

When I had seen the way Hugo had looked at George's body, then felt the cumulative horrors of Lisa and June's deaths pressing on me, and the way Stanley had been so blasé about killing both June and Freddy—just a regular evening's work to him—it made me finally realise what kind of man he really was, and it was then I felt able to fire that little pistol. It was then I felt I had a duty to fire it.

I've still got it, hidden away, only one bullet left in it now, though I don't doubt Hugo could get more if I asked. If I have learned one thing from my adventures, it's that you never know when you might need a weapon. The knife from the cave episode was still in the cave somewhere, along with the lighter, but the gun… I would keep that safe, just in case my curse moves me to need it again.

Was I scared the lads or even the cat would succumb to the curse?

No, Misty still had eight of her nine lives, and Hugo and George were tough little gits who would protect me as fiercely as they had each other. I felt safe with them and could only hope they'd be safe with me.

'On the bright side,' I thought, feeling my death-defying humour begin to re-emerge, 'Little Kerton-on-Sea's going to be really popular this summer. After all those bodies turning up everywhere, it might have the biggest tourist boom ever… Every cloud, as they say.'

We hit the A35 minutes later. "Bus ho!" Hugo said with a gleeful air punch as he drove the three of us, battered and bruised in our bodies and hearts, on to a new adventure.

The End

About The Author

J.D. Warner is a poet and writer, who has spent her life reading and writing quirky stories in fantasy and sci-fi worlds. A lifelong geology nerd, she also keeps Amazon parrots, who sometimes bite to remind her she lives in the real world.

In 2000, her sci-fi epic serial Another Side of the Sky ran for a year in Keep It Coming Magazine, and in 2019 she released the fantasy novel Hex-Tych, to good reviews. Her short stories appear in various publications and she was once a winner in the short story contest held at The Cheltenham Literary Festival.

Also by J.D. Warner

The
Hartpury
Horror

Molly Turner Trilogy, Book 1
(The Unseeing Eye, 2021)

WHEN CRIMINALS MAKE their money-drop in the quiet village of Hartpury, litter-collecting pensioner Molly Turner finds it. Being a frightfully honest lady, she leaves the bag well alone, but the money goes missing and Molly is suspected. A hunt ensues and, as the bad guys torment old Molly (who refuses to be old), she has to fight through her own past trauma to survive the search.

ISBN 978-9916-4-0291-7 (paperback)
ISBN 978-9916-9-5891-9 (Kindle)

Lightning Source UK Ltd.
Milton Keynes UK
UKHW012157111221
395505UK00001B/40

9 789916 958964